Reborn
Blood Courtesans 1
Vampire Romance

Michelle Fox

Copyright © 2016 Michelle Fox

All rights reserved.

WELCOME TO THE SHADOW WORLD...

I have to sell myself to the vampires. I know it's not safe, but there's no other option. Not for the amount of money I need. It's either become a blood courtesan or watch my mom die while we lose the only home I've ever known.

So I leap before I look and soon I'm sharing a bed with vampire Kristos Anastos. He's hot, rich and his fangs hurt so good. The courtesan thing is better than I thought it would be...until bullets start to fly.

Kristos believes he's the target, but it soon becomes clear it's not him they're after. It's me. And if I want to live, I'd better figure out why.

I thought I was just a college student, a good kid raised by a single mom down on her luck, but I have secrets even I don't know about.

Blood is money and mine may be worth the most of all.

Full length novel with NO cliffhanger. Previously published as Blood Struck and revised and expanded in this new edition for an even more fangalicious read.

What readers say...

"Kept me turning the pages to see what twists and turns were going to happen next . ABSOLUTELY LOVE the intriguing intricacies of her creative writing about the vampires."

"Please make more vampire books like this I loved it. What I like about this book is there is a good story behind it. Its not just vampires killing humans. I love when there is that one vampire that falls so in life with a human woman that he will risk his own life for her and go against his own rules just to save her and keep her for himself. And this book gives us readers that and more. If you have not read this book read it!!! This book was so good I loved it!"

"Incredibly likable characters. Snarky dialogue. Adventure. Gunfire. Vile bad guys. Smoldering hot hero. Funny, sweet heroine. Kidnapping. Daring rescues. Steamy sex. Happy ending. This story has it all. Loved it!"

ACKNOWLEDGMENTS

With many thanks and much love to my readers and to all lovers of fangs out there!

1

Be sure to check out the other books in the series at http://www.bloodcourtesans.com.

***

"What is it that interests you in becoming a courtesan to vampires?" Madame Rouge watched me, assessing. She had the beauty most women would kill for; tall, slender and an oval face with lush, red lips and crystal blue eyes topped off with impossibly long lashes. Her caramel brown hair was pulled up in a bun with long curls spilling down to her shoulders. She was younger than I'd expected with a somewhat archaic manner of speaking. And now she wanted me to explain what it was that made selling my body to vampires my number one career choice.

Why would a girl from the backwoods of New York state travel to its glittering capital, New York City, just to sell her body?

I shifted in my chair and tugged the hem of my skirt down to make sure it covered my knees. Her oxblood lips curled in amusement at the movement and I froze, realizing it was a mistake.

Job hunting tip number one: When applying for a job as a courtesan, demure modesty was not an asset.

A long silence ensued because I didn't know how to tell her what she wanted to hear. This job was my one shot to get the expensive not-covered-by-insurance medical care that could cure my mom and keep my childhood home. I was a classic sob story who needed a large amount of cash *fast*, but I didn't want pity. I was pretty sure it wasn't a turn-on in the world I sought to join.

"Miss Danson?" she prompted. Her body language disengaged from our interview. She no longer leaned forward and she dropped my resume on her desk. A resume that said nothing much about me beyond I was a college student who'd held a string of low paying part-time gigs as I worked my way through school.

"Call me Myra," I said uncomfortable with her formal address. "I need the money. And, I, uh, like sex." It's not a lie if you really do like something you've never done, right? The theory sounded great to me, I just had no idea how things worked on a practical level. I hadn't dated a lot, dividing my attention between college and tending to my mother left little time to socialize.

She put her hand back on my application. "Clara said you were experienced, which is why I even agreed to meet with you. I need girls who aren't afraid of sex and know how to enjoy themselves. The vampires demand it."

I bit back a laugh at the mention of my old high school 'frenemy'. She hated me. If I hadn't known it before, I knew it now because she was lying, purposely setting me up for a fall. I'd told her nothing about my alleged 'experience' only asked her how to get in touch with Madame Rouge. Anything else she made up just to screw with me.

Focusing back on Madame Rouge, I smiled brightly. "I love sex, sex loves me." Fake it until you make it, right?

She nodded. "Good. Shrinking violets don't taste good and vampires don't want hysterical girls who run screaming to the police." She looked at my application again. "You've never slept with a vampire?"

I shook my head.

This pleased Madame and she smiled. "That raises your price." At my confused look, she explained, "No scarring at the neck. You're fresh meat."

I flushed at her phrasing and she laughed. "They find blushing sexy. You'll be very popular with that fair skin of yours showing every emotion." She quickly scanned through my application one last time before saying, "I think you'll do. When can you start?"

"As soon as possible." I was on a deadline. I'd given myself a week to do this, figuring I could miss that much class and still pass. I just hoped it was enough time to raise the money I needed.

She smiled at me again, pleased. "Excellent. How does tonight sound?"

"Tonight?" I repeated, my voice squeaking. "I don't have any clothes." Or time to find someone to deflower me quick so I didn't lose my virginity and get the blood sucked out of me on the same night.

"We have an extensive closet here for just such an occasion." She pushed a button on her phone. "Jacques, please bring three outfits with Kristos in mind to my office."

A moment later, a guy I assumed was Jacques stalked into the office in a shock of pink hair and tight neon green jeans. His mesh tank top displayed a lean, defined frame and left nothing to the imagination. "Make way for fashion, ladies," he said in a high trill. In his arms, he carried a jumble of clothes which he arranged into outfits on the back of the couch that sat along the far wall of Madame Rouge's spacious office.

The clothes he'd brought looked small and way too revealing. I found myself tugging on the hem of my skirt again, anxious at the thought of exposing so much skin.

Madame Rouge waved her hand, the motion languid and elegant. "Jacques meet Myra. She'll be going out for an audition tonight."

Jacques sighed and looked down his nose at me. He didn't speak, just sniffed and then resumed fussing over the clothes he'd brought in.

"Nice to meet you," I said, trying to be polite.

"Yeah, sure." He flicked his wrist in my general direction. Then, holding up a yellow dress, he asked, "What about this one?"

"I prefer the blue for her. She's perfect for jewel tones with her alabaster skin and auburn hair." Madame picked up a blue corset and a skinny band of leather that was supposed to be a skirt. "But the pink might be good too." The pink in question was a go-go hooker look consisting of a latex mini dress with matching thigh-high boots. She turned to me, focusing those impossibly clear blue eyes on me, lashes all aflutter. "What do you think, Miss Danson?"

"I think none of that is anything fresh meat would wear," I said, blurting out my gut reaction. It all looked cheap and tawdry to me and yeah, I was selling my body, but I had some standards thank-you-very-much. I was not vampire bait Barbie. Assuming I had any say in the matter. While I would do anything for my mom, I wouldn't go along to get along either.

Madame Rouge didn't seem too upset by my blunt response, but Jacques stiffened and glared at me with narrowed eyes.

She fingered the pink latex and then let it go with a small sigh. "It's all very fashionable, but she has a point, I think. Do we have anything more romantic, more flow-y?"

Jacques huffed and gathered up the clothes. "I'll be right back." He left the room, his cowboy boots making a thudding sound despite the plush carpet.

"Sorry," I called after him with an apologetic look to Madame Rouge. Note to self: Try not to piss everyone off on your first day on the job.

Madam Rouge just laughed, a sweet musical sound that probably made birds burn with envy. She was a mesmerizing concoction of feminine perfection and I felt like Bertha the fat, hippy and hairy next to her. "No worries, my dear. I like a girl who has a vision of her brand."

"Brand?"

She went to her desk. "Yes, you are a product and how you package yourself determines how well you'll sell." She typed something on her computer and turned the screen so I could see. "We set up web pages for each of our girls. We do a pictorial and a bio targeting certain tastes and experiences. We like to offer clients a variety of pleasures."

I leaned in and looked at the page. The girl featured was a blonde named Victoria. She wore a bra that exposed her pink nipples and a barely there thong. Her bio stated she "tasted great with champagne."

What does that even mean?

Jacques bustled into the room with a blasé, "I'm back. What do you think of this?"

I turned and my jaw dropped at the sight of the dress in his hands. It was a sapphire blue floor length gown in a shiny fabric that looked to be silk. The halter-top had a plunging neckline so deep, I wondered if it would reveal my belly button. He turned it around to show the dress was backless and then flipped back to the front to display the slit that went straight up the middle of the skirt.

"Stunning. You have the best taste," Madame Rouge said, her voice warm with appreciation. "Miss Danson?"

"It's beautiful," I breathed, reaching out to touch it.

Jacques smiled, pleased with himself and pulled the dress back until it was just out of reach. "I brought some lace thigh-highs to go with it. The slit allows you to play peek-a-boo if you wish."

Peek-a-boo?

"That is an excellent detail," Madame Rouge said. Noting my confusion, she smiled. "Our clients appreciate a little tease. You might think of signing up for a burlesque seminar at some point to hone those skills. Great sex is all about anticipation."

Jacques sniffed and looked over my navy interview suit. "Take off those rags you're abusing the public eye with and let's see how this looks."

I flushed at the thought of disrobing in front of them, but noting Madame Rouge's expectant look, I realized this must be some unspoken test. If you're going to have sex and engage in bloodletting for a living, I guess you can't be shy about getting naked. If your boss wants to see the goods, you show the goods.

Resigned, I shrugged out of my jacket and slipped off the lace camisole I wore underneath. Leaving my bra on for the moment, I unzipped and wiggled out of my skirt.

"Oh my God, you're wearing mass market underwear," Jacques said, disgust filling his voice.

My blush deepened and spread to my chest. Madam Rouge clasped her hands together, almost applauding. "Oh very, nice Miss Danson. I don't think we have anyone who blushes quite like you on staff." To Jacques she said, "Be nice. We can't all have your exquisite taste."

Jacques gave a petulant 'humph' and stared at my underwear as if willing it off my body. When I reached for the dress, he jumped back. "Oh no, not with that made-in-China sweatshop underwear on your body. It comes off or the dress does not go on, honey."

"Do you have something I can wear?" I asked.

He held up a finger and wagged it at me. "First, there is no bra with this dress. Second, underwear never comes back so we don't supply it."

Go commando? I looked at Madame Rouge who raised a perfectly contoured eyebrow. With a sigh I unhooked my bra and tossed it into the pile with the rest of my clothes. Then I slipped off my underwear. There, I was naked. *Ta-dah.*

Madame Rouge took the opportunity to walk around me. "Very nice." She ran a hand down my back, raising goose bumps as she went. "Soft skin, no marks or blemishes. Oh, they'll love you." She stepped in front of me, gaze assessing my chest. "Large, firm breasts. A surprise since your frame is so slight." She paused to heft a breast in her hand, fingers grazing the tip. When it puckered at her touch, she gave a nod of approval. "Let's see how the dress looks."

Jacques dropped the dress over my head and arranged it on my body with confident expertise. The neckline plunged almost to my belly button and the key to keeping my breasts covered was tying the halter tight behind my neck. The slit stopped about six inches before my pubic mound. I would have to be careful when I walked or my vagina would play peek-a-boo with everyone I met.

Yikes.

"Here, put these on and we'll see how it comes together." Jacques handed me the thigh highs.

They were a sheer black with lace on the top. Very feminine. I pulled them on while Jacques rummaged in a large wardrobe behind Madame Rouge's desk. When he emerged, he handed me a pair of blue mules with kitten heels. I slipped my feet into the shoes and then stood up.

Spinning in a slow circle, my arms open, I asked, "What do you think?"

"You need a different hair-do," Madame Rouge said. "But otherwise, I think the dress suits you." She went back to her phone and dialed. "Savon, we need your skills."

Jacques scooped up my suit and underwear. "I'm going to burn these."

"What? Those are my clothes!" I reached for them, wanting to take them back.

He stepped back, tightening his grip on my clothes. "Honey, when you get your first paycheck, these won't even be good enough to use as cleaning rags. Trust me, you're not the first girl I've dressed."

I slowly lowered my hand, giving up on getting my clothes back. "What will I wear home?"

"You can keep the dress. We'll deduct it from your paycheck," Madame Rouge said.

Jacques shot an arch look at Madame Rouge. "Besides, are you really saying that you are so attached to a navy suit, which is the height of generic? Because, if so, I suggest Madame reconsider your suitability for this work. There is nothing generic about what we do here."

What could I say to that? Nothing. So I let him go and take my clothes with him.

"Jacques knows how to make girls look their best. If you can stand it, take him shopping to set up a work wardrobe," Madame Rouge said with a kind smile. "He has a heart of gold, if you can get past his sarcasm. He'll never steer you wrong when it comes to clothes. I wouldn't put up with him otherwise."

"But of course, I am your favorite," said an amused masculine voice with a French accent.

I turned to see a tall, blond man step into the office. In contrast to Jacques' flamboyance, he wore all black, which looked severe against his pale complexion.

He entered the room with an airy, "I'm Savon. I do the hair and make-up." He set a large make-up case on the floor and opened it to pull out a hair brush and dryer. "Sit down, *s'il vous plait*."

I sat in one of the office chairs, carefully arranging the dress so I didn't flash anyone. Savon fluffed my hair around my shoulders. "Not too fine, not too thick. Your hair is just right. Is this your natural color?"

"Yes," I said.

"Lovely." He ran the brush through my hair, tugging through some snarls.

"Thanks."

Ten minutes later I'd been brushed, moussed and blow dried into a 'down do' full of swirling body. Savon handed me a mirror so I could see the result and I gasped. "I look like I should be in a Pantene commercial."

He laughed. "*Oui*, of course you do. I did your hair, didn't I?" At my nod of agreement, he said, "Now let's do some make-up."

"Just the eyes and lips, Savon. We don't want to hide that blush of hers," Madame Rouge said looking up from her computer. She had returned to her desk and busied herself typing while Savon worked his magic.

"*Absolutement*, Madame," he murmured in response as he looked through his make-up case. Brandishing a pair of tweezers, he said, "Your skin is like fine porcelain, to cover it with anything would be a sin." With a deft touch, he plucked my eyebrows.

I winced and asked, "Have you worked here long?" What I really wanted to know was how someone ended up with a career making up courtesans, but I wasn't brave enough to say it so bluntly.

"Years and years." He dropped the tweezers back in his case and selected an eye shadow palette. He did a quick application of eye shadow followed by liner and mascara. The final touch was a subtle lipstick. As he worked, I caught glimpses of myself in the small mirror attached to his make-up case. The lipstick shade matched my natural lip color, giving it just a little something extra.

"You're all set, mademoiselle," he said cleaning up his supplies. "What does Madame think?"

Madame Rouge gestured for me to stand and I did another spin to show off the complete look.

"You are a lovely young woman, Miss Danson."

"Yes, really divine." Savon nodded in agreement.

I blushed and looked at my feet. She had to be joking. I doubted I looked as gorgeous as Madame.

"Are you unconvinced?" Madame Rouge stood up and pulled out a floor length mirror hidden in a clever compartment behind the bookcase on the side wall.

The woman who looked back at me was tall and model pretty. My eyelashes were almost as long as Madame's now and there was a pink glow to my skin. You would never know I had fat pants at home. Or that my idea of dressing up was wearing clean jeans with a Hard Rock Cafe T-shirt from my senior year trip to London.

Somehow I'd been transformed into the supermodel fantasy version of myself. I had thought that would take plastic surgery, but really all I ever needed was the right dress and make-up. *Huh. Go figure.*

"Thank you, Savon. I love what you did with my hair." I put a hand to my head in wonder. He'd artfully tousled my locks into a sexy bed head.

"It's easy to make good hair look great," he said with a smile and giving a little bow. "Now, Madame, if you are done with me, I will go, *oui?*"

"*Mais oui. Merci, monsieur.*" She gave him a distracted wave as he left. Then, pulling a camera out of a desk drawer she said, "We need to take a picture for Kristos' approval."

I put a hand to my head. This was all going so fast. I couldn't keep up. "Who is Kristos?"

"Your trainer and first client. He's an affluent man and he loves girls like you, elegant yet passionate. Plus, the fresher the better. Maybe you didn't just fall off the turnip truck, but it wasn't that long ago either." She led me to an empty spot along the wall of her office. "Why don't you give me a few different poses?"

I smiled and clasped my hands behind my back.

She lowered the camera, shaking her head. "This is not a school picture, my dear. Remember your brand."

My brand. Right. The virgin pretending she knew something. I slipped one leg in front of the other, stuck my chest out and tried to pout like Marilyn Monroe.

She sighed and lowered the camera. "You look constipated."

"Sorry. I don't really know what I'm doing." I could feel the hot flush of bewildered embarrassment creeping up my neck.

"Yes, I can tell." She walked over to me and pulled my arm overhead. "Put your arm up like this and look at it as if you are reaching for the most delicious chocolate. The leg should stay in front like you have it and then let your other hand trail down your neck between your breasts. Okay? Now, don't move."

She snapped several pictures like that and then asked me to turn around and look over my shoulder. "That will work, I think. Let me just email these to Kristos for his approval."

She inserted the memory card into the computer and downloaded the pictures, quickly selecting the two best ones to attach to an email she had already written. I read over her shoulder as she worked.

Kristos:

I have a fresh one for you. Experienced, but barely. Never been blooded and very sweet. She blushes easily. I would guess she would go well with a Bordeaux or port brandy, but would like your thoughts on that once you've had a taste. As always, I trust you will go gently with her audition.

Send a car if she meets your approval. She's here in my office waiting.

Regards,

Madame Rouge

Once the email had been sent, Madame Rouge turned to me, her gaze settling on me with palpable weight. "So, let's discuss the rules. Your job is to please the client. You back sell behind my back and you'll be out of a job."

I blinked in confusion. "Back sell?"

"Try to negotiate your services directly. Going out on your own is more dangerous than you know." She crossed her arms and leaned back in her chair. "I offer a certain level of protection to my girls. Our clients pay a membership fee and they know to behave if they want to stay in my good graces. You go it alone and there's nothing to stop them."

I put a hand to my throat. "Are vampires that dangerous?" Had I just made a mistake? We knew so little beyond the fact that they existed. They lived hidden, shadowed lives and humans seemed content to keep it that way.

She watched my hand, eyes gleaming with what appeared to be amusement. "Not generally, but living as long as they have sometimes changes them in a bad way. Or their original time period may have engaged in practices we no longer find acceptable today. I spend a lot of time ensuring clients can be trusted and that they understand the terms of service. When you work with me, you know you'll come home safe."

I cleared my throat as I processed everything she'd just explained. "So you said I am to please the client, what does that mean? Can I say no to anything?"

"You can say no, but I would not make a habit of it if you want to make money. This is no job for prudes. Kristos will be a good introduction to what this work entails. You'll know after tonight if this is for you."

Her computer gave a soft ding signaling that a new email had arrived. She checked it and nodded in satisfaction. "Kristos approves. He's sending a car."

At that, my heart began to race as I realized this was really happening. Madame Rouge either didn't notice or overlooked my shell-shocked reaction and handed me a stack of papers.

"This is your contract. It includes a non-disclosure agreement and outlines payment terms. Also, you'll see that, if your trainer's evaluation is poor, we reserve the right to dissolve our relationship with you." She flipped through the pages, marking an X where I needed to sign. "In other words, do what Kristos says. He's trained other girls and he knows what he's doing. Impress him and you impress me, which means more clients for you. Understood?" She gave me an expectant look.

I managed a nod as she handed the contract over to me. I tried to read the twisted legalese as I signed, but lacked the mental clarity to focus on the words. Images of what Kristos might look like and what it would be like to let him feed on me consumed my mind. My nerves were on high alert and my hands shook as I made my way through the pages, signing and initialing where she indicated.

When I finally finished, Madame Rouge gave me a bright smile. "Congratulations. You are officially a blood courtesan."

2

On the limo ride to meet Kristos, I sent a quick text to my mom letting her know I would be in the city at least overnight, if not for a few more days. My dad had ditched us both long before I was born and the abandonment made my mom and I close. I knew she'd worry if I didn't check in. I'd told her I had a job interview, which was mostly true, although I'd led her to believe it was for a corporate internship that would look good on my graduate school application.

She was just recovering from her last chemo treatment and didn't need any extra stress. Not that I would, in a million years, tell her about what I was doing. No point in saving her from cancer only to kill her with my loose morals. As far as I was concerned, what happened in New York was going to stay there.

It only took a minute to check in with mom and I was left with way too much time to think. First, about my Dad. Would things be different if he was around? I'd learned early on to push him to the back of my mind because I didn't believe in dwelling on things that couldn't be changed. With mom so sick, though, I felt his abandonment of us as a new loss.

Then I thought about sex. About vampires. About how the hell I was going to pull this blood courtesan thing off. I was so out of my league I was on another planet.

I'd never met a vampire. Sure, maybe seen one or two from afar, but that was it. Our society had transferred the 'don't ask don't tell' policy from gays to supernaturals. We didn't know what was out there and we were good with it. If we had to know, fine. Like the time there had been a vampire serial killer. Or when another one set up a big philanthropic foundation for his descendants. Beyond those news bites, I went through my life as if everyone around me was human and so did everybody else.

These were the things I did know: Vampires liked blushing and there was some kind of alcohol connection. Oh and I was about to allow them to suck my blood during sex. That was already too much information.

Fear of the unknown overwhelmed me, and by the time the limo dropped me off at a swanky restaurant named Taos, I was about ready to bolt. I never had the chance though, because a cadre of muscle-bound guards swarmed me, their expressions grim. It was early fall and still warm, but a chill went through me. This was the point of no return. There was no going back. I hugged myself, wishing I'd thought to ask for a wrap.

"Miss Danson?" asked a blond man with a buzz cut and a broken-one-time-too-many nose. Sunglasses hid his eyes and his black suit was identical to the rest of his group.

At my nod, the men closed rank around me and hustled me toward my fate. One of them even shoved me along when I paused to pull the hem of my dress off my heel.

"Is that really necessary?" I asked, stumbling. The gown was just a little too long or my heels were just a little too short. Either way, the result was the same; the mere act of walking was complicated. Worse, a game of crotch peek-a-boo threatened to break out at any second and I had to pay close attention to how I moved in order to keep the goods under wraps.

"Standard security precautions, Miss Danson."

"Well, can we go a little slower? I'm wearing heels you know," I snapped.

They slowed for about two seconds, whisking me through the entrance and to the dining room. The restaurant was dimly lit with candles on every table and a Zen-like minimalist decor in a mix of beige and black tones. A tuxedo clad maître d' stood behind a marble-topped bar at the entrance. He glanced up as we crossed the threshold. In fact, judging from the abrupt silence that met my arrival, *everyone* noticed our appearance. How could they miss it? I was a woman in a very fancy dress surrounded by what looked like a Navy Seal special ops team.

Hoping to spot Kristos before he saw me, I scanned the dining room as we passed through the entry way and into the large dining room. I wanted to give myself some time to prepare mentally. The restaurant was full of couples and double dates.

Everyone appeared to be matched with a partner. Aside from curious stares and speculative gawking, no one seemed to be looking for me specifically.

By then the security detail had sped up again, herding me through the restaurant like an errant lamb. I struggled not to trip as my dress twined around my legs and under my heels. *Stupid slit.*

"There he is. Nine o'clock," said one of the guards to the others.

I turned to look and saw him. Kristos the vampire took my breath away. In a room full of noise and movement, he was motionless. His absolute stillness made him stand out in sharp relief, timeless as ancient statue. I studied his features, noting the hooked nose and square jaw. His shoulders were broad and his suit followed the trim muscle of his physique. As far as I knew it was the first time I'd ever seen a vampire up close and personal, and he was much better looking than I had anticipated.

For some unknown reason, I was instantly attracted to him, and the moment I had that insight he moved, turning his head to focus on me. For a long second, everything and everyone around me ceased to exist, it was just me and Kristos. My pulse quickened and my breathing came fast. I felt like I was falling into his gaze, as if his eyes were swallowing me whole and then....and then I was on the floor, my dress finally bringing me down.

With a loud *'oof'* I slammed to the ground, trying to land on my side to avoid face planting. The momentum rolled me onto my back, whipping my legs apart, which displayed my lack of underwear for all to see.

There was a moment of silence before a sonic wave of gasps and titters crashed down on me, bringing my humiliation to the fore. The security guys just stood there, apparently just as shocked as everyone else that I had a real live vagina under my dress.

Burning with mortification, I quickly pulled the gown over my naked bits and tried to stand up, but the heels caught in the hem again.

Damn it.

The guards still hadn't moved either. Not one of them lifted a finger to help me. Useless bastard Navy Seal poseurs.

So I crawled. Kristos' table wasn't that far away and it was a large round with a long table cloth. My goal was to get under there and hide until I was dead and mummified beyond recognition.

People murmured as I passed their tables, but I ignored it, focusing with tunnel vision on just getting to Kristos' table without flashing anyone else.

Once I was there, I bolted into my hidey-hole, huddling with my knees pulled up to my chest and my skirt wrapped around me like a cocoon. Sniffing back tears, I squeezed my eyes closed and tried to pretend none of this was happening.

Oh, how far the fantasy supermodel version of me had fallen. Right into hell.

"Miss Danson?" Kristos ducked under the table to peer at

me, curiosity gleaming in his eyes. Now that we were face-to-face I could see they were light aquamarine blue.

"Go away," I sniffed.

"After that entrance, I can't possibly leave you alone." He slipped under the table with me, which just made me cry harder. "Are you all right? I mean, physically as your emotional distress is obvious." He laid a gentle hand on my shoulder.

I nodded. "I'm fine. It's just these damn shoes. They kept tripping me up and your guards wouldn't slow down." I kicked off the shoes in question. I never wanted to wear them again.

"Excuse me a moment," Kristos said. "I'll be right back."

The tears welled up in my eyes again. He was probably calling Madame Rouge and telling her to fire me. My courtesan career would end before it even started. Without that money, cancer would kill my mom. I stifled a loud sob at the thought.

Beyond the table, I heard deep voices muttering. One of them sounded very upset, going deeper and louder than the others.

Then Kristos was back, this time with a bottle of wine and a cheese plate. "Would you like something to drink or eat?" Concern for me shone in his eyes. I had mostly stopped crying by then, but his pity started me up again.

I sniffed. "Wine sounds good." Maybe if I got drunk things would improve.

He handed me a glass and I drained it, not even tasting the wine. When I held up my glass for more, he shook his head. "I don't want you drinking recklessly. How about some cheese so the wine doesn't go to your head?"

I frowned and snatched the bottle from his hand. "Listen, more people just saw my vagina than I've slept with in my whole life. I royally flubbed my first night at a new job. I think I'm entitled to a little reckless drinking thank-you-very-much." With that, I chugged directly from the bottle, greedy for oblivion.

Kristos pulled the bottle from my hands with a 'tsk' of disapproval. "I realize the night has not gone as planned, but I would prefer not to let one minor incident ruin the whole evening. Why don't we sit at the table and start over?"

With all those people out there that had seen my *va-jay-jay?* Humiliation burned through me again. I couldn't face it. "I thought I would stay here for a while, until--"

Kristos interrupted and said, "Everyone has gone?" He smiled and I stopped breathing because, even through my haze of mortification, I could appreciate that he was beautiful. "They are already gone. I had them escorted out."

I gaped at him. So that was what money and power was good for. Clearing out restaurants just on your say so. "They let you do that?"

He shrugged. "Of course. I own the restaurant."

I poked my head out from under the table and indeed the restaurant was empty, except for the security detail, which congregated in the small foyer at the front of the restaurant. They weren't even looking my way. Most of them were preoccupied with their smart phones while two of them watched the front door, their backs to me.

Well, then. This I can handle.

We sat at the table and I placed my napkin in my lap, grateful for the impromptu loin cloth. Next time I picked out a swanky dress I would have underwear or select one that wouldn't cause me to flash everyone in the room. Live and learn, right?

"Let's start over, shall we?" Kristos offered me his hand. "I'm Kristos."

I took his hand with a shy smile. Oh, what he must think of me. Horrible things I was sure. He was just being nice given that I was new. Most people cut someone slack if it was their first day on the job. "Hi, I'm Myra and I'm not wearing any panties."

He laughed at that. "I saw. It was a nice view."

I blushed.

He watched, transfixed as it flamed over my cheeks and down my neck. I peeked down to see that, yep, my chest was overly pink too.

"Lovely," he breathed, reaching out to trace my collar bone with his finger. There was a hunger in his eyes that warned me to be still and not make any sudden movements.

A waiter cleared his throat as he set plates of food in front of me. "Your order, miss."

Kristos leaned back in his chair, the intensity between us dissipating as he did so.

"This is a lot of food," I said, wondering how I would eat it all. There was a plate of pasta with marinara and a surf n' turf platter with one of the largest lobster tails I'd ever seen. In addition, the waiter set down three different appetizers and a salad of mixed greens.

"I asked the kitchen to make up a few different plates using what they already had in process. You don't mind?"

I shook my head. "No, not as long as you don't expect me to eat it all. I mean, it looks delicious, but my stomach is only so big, you know?"

He nodded. "Pick what pleases you most."

I pulled the lobster toward me, moving the other plates out of the way. My stomach growled reminding me I hadn't eaten in a very long time.

"Has Madame Rouge been starving you?" he asked as my stomach broadcasted its status.

Embarrassment burned my cheeks. "It's just been a very busy day."

His eyes were riveted on my skin, watching the progression of my blush. "I understand she hired you just today."

I nodded, my mouth too full of succulent lobster to talk.

"What makes this work attractive to you?"

"Why do you ask?" I asked once I had swallowed.

"I like to understand people's motivations," he said.

"I need the money. No baser motivation than that," I said, deciding I may as well be honest. After all he wasn't buying me dinner pretending we were going to get married someday.

"For what? School? A car? Clothes?" His eyes caught mine

and pinned me down, shining with open curiosity.

I shook my head and looked down at my plate as sadness threatened to overwhelm me. "My mom has cancer." Why had I told him that? The last thing I wanted was pity.

He reached over, tilting my chin up to meet his gaze again. "That's a very noble motivation, Myra."

I bit my lip. His eyes were disconcerting, his gaze palpable. "I guess."

Kristos put his thumb on my bottom lip and gently pulled it out from under my teeth. "You don't want to talk about it?"

"I don't want you to feel sorry for me. It makes it all worse somehow," I said, my eyes hot with more tears. *Would I ever stop crying in front of this guy?*

Seeing how close to the surface my emotions ran on that topic, he changed the subject. "You said my guards were too fast?"

"I just couldn't keep up with this dress and those shoes," I said, relieved to not be focusing on my mom. "I asked them to slow down, but they just went faster."

A muscle in his cheek throbbed as he clenched his jaw. "I want you to know that is unacceptable."

"I'm sorry," I said, flustered. "I won't ask them to slow down again."

"No, Myra, I'm talking about them. They should have taken more care with you." He laid a hand on my arm, thumb caressing my skin, the contact sending shivers down my spine. From a distance he was handsome, but up close he smoldered hot enough to steal the oxygen from the air. "I don't want you to think their treatment of you represents me."

"You've been nothing but kind," I stammered. "I thought you would have sent me back already."

"Not after you made such an interesting entrance." He withdrew his hand and I found myself missing the contact. "You're blushing again. You really are quite sensitive, Madame Rouge did not overstate on that point."

"Sorry."

"Don't apologize. It's beautiful. You're very lovely, Myra." He lifted my free hand to his lips, pressing them against my palm in a moist kiss. "I can't wait to see how far below your dress that blush goes."

Not knowing what to say to that, I shoved more lobster in my mouth. In my chest, my heart began pounding, fast and furious.

Kristos scooted his chair closer to mine and leaned in to plant a soft kiss on my neck. I froze and then my heart began to beat triple time. "Would you mind if I had a quick taste?" he asked, whispering in my ear.

His closeness pulled at something deep inside me and goose bumps danced across my skin, tightening my nipples. *Oh my God, I'm turned on*, I realized with some surprise. Maybe losing my virginity to a vampire would be more fun than I had thought. Maybe all my Type-A anxiety was for nothing.

Closing my eyes and swallowing hard, I said, "Please help yourself." *Gah.* So not classy. It sounded like I was welcoming him to the all-you-can-suck blood buffet.

"Thank you. I would have been sad if you said no." He kissed my neck again and made his way down to my collarbone, pulling my skin into his mouth with gentle suction. One hand kneaded my back while the other inched its way toward the juncture of my thighs.

Fear mingling with desire, I slipped my hands underneath my legs to keep from moving to stop him. I would get used to this, I promised myself. It was just first-time nerves. It helped that he was not only gorgeous, but also experienced. The better it felt, the easier this would be.

When the bite came, I gasped and threw my head back. It hurt, but it was more than pain, there was an unexpected pleasure to its sting too. Between my legs, his fingers found me wet and the longer he sucked at the bite, the more I squirmed, wanting something more.

He pulled away from my neck and removed his hand from under my skirt. His eyes were dark with desire while mine were wide with shock. "Madame Rouge was right, you are good with Bordeaux," he said. "And there's something else there, something I can't quite place. What is your lineage?"

"My what?" I moved to rearrange the napkin over my lap, still uncomfortable with how much skin the dress exposed. The simple movement caused him to abandon his question.

Frowning, Kristos reached over and tugged the napkin away from me. "I'd rather you not. I like the view." He leaned in close once more. This time my mouth was the target. Hungry lips crushed mine in a scorching kiss that made my toes curl. His fingers returned to the bud at my core and I shivered as pleasure pressed against my inner walls, just moments away from a climax.

In the back of my mind, I worried about the security guards. Public sex had never been one of my fantasies, but there I was being felt up and kissed with such finesse it sounded like a grand idea. I didn't want him to stop. Maybe it was the bite or maybe it was because he was a vampire. Either way my flesh ached for him. I needed him to touch me. Any fear I'd felt gave way to a hot desire.

Kristos deepened our kiss, slipping his tongue between my lips as his free hand went to cradle the back of my head. His other hand began to move faster and I sighed as my body quickened with him. I gave a soft cry into his mouth when I came. Pleasure rushed the nexus of my legs, leaving me warm and tingling.

Kristos smiled against my lips and then broke contact as he returned to his seat.

A little frazzled by what had just transpired, I grabbed my wine glass and gulped the fruity liquid down. As I moved to set it on the table after draining it dry, it exploded in my hand with a sharp crack.

I never heard the bullet. Or maybe I did, but failed to understand the significance of the sound. All I knew was my glass shattered, spraying wine and shrapnel into my palm and at my face.

I shrieked and dropped the glass, my other hand moving up to shield my head. The swish of wind overhead signaled the addition of arrows to the artillery raining down on the restaurant. They buried themselves in the wall with vibrating 'thunks.'

Kristos dropped to the floor, yanking me down with him. His eyes scanned the restaurant as bullets whined over our heads to thud into the wall behind us. "We have to get out of here."

I heard his words and agreed wholeheartedly with his assessment, but couldn't respond. I was transfixed by my hand which welled blood in deep maroon. Lots of blood. *So* much blood.

"Myra?" He gave me a little shake and then went flat on the floor as another arrow sailed over us, this one low enough I could have reached up and touched it as it flew by.

I blinked at him, knowing I should listen to him, that what he said was important, but I couldn't focus. Kristos seemed to sense my shock because he grabbed me by the shoulders and shoved me toward the kitchen as more bullets zipped through the air above us.

I watched my blood drip on the floor as we went, feeling increasing panic at the amount of it. "What is going on?" I had to yell to be heard over all the bullets and the sound of glass shattering as they hit the heavy chandeliers overhead.

"Nothing good. Beyond that I don't know." Kristos pulled me through the kitchen, which had already been abandoned, to a back door and scanned the alley way outside. "Here, we'll go out this way." He glanced down at my bare feet. "Can you manage?"

"Yes," I said. Those shoes were a menace. Wearing them while running from gunmen didn't seem like a path to continued good health.

"Don't panic if I run faster than you. I'm the target, you'll be safer without me next to you. I'll get a car and come back to pick you up, understood?"

I nodded and then we were in the alley. At first, it was quiet and it seemed like maybe we would get away safely, but then bullets started pinging off the brick walls. I flinched each time one hit, but kept running. As he'd warned, Kristos rapidly outpaced me, moving so fast he was a blur. I tried to stick to shadows, grateful my dress was blue and not yellow. However, I knew my fair skin stood out in the dark, making me easy to spot.

I ran and tried not to think about what it would feel like to have a bullet smash into my exposed back. At the end of the alley was a busy street with lots of people. If I could just make it there I might be safe or find a cop even. Bullets dogged me every step of the way, showering me with shards of shattered brick. Why anyone would work so hard to shoot me, didn't make any sense to me. Couldn't they see Kristos wasn't there?

At one point, I whirled around and screamed, "Kristos is gone. I'm really not worth shooting."

A shadowy figure at the other end of the alley paused briefly and the bullets stopped flying for all of five seconds before coming faster than ever. Kristos had been wrong, I wasn't safer without him, I was in more danger. I picked up the pace, widening my stride into a full sprint, rough pavement scraping my feet.

Just as I reached the end of the alley, a bullet narrowly missed my head and drove sharp bits of brick into my arm and neck as it hit the wall. The brick ripped through my skin and hot blood rolled down my arm. At the same time, a squeal of tires announced the arrival of a silver sports car. The car stopped inches from taking me out at the kneecaps.

Kristos stuck his head out the driver's window and shouted, "Get in."

One hand clamped on my shoulder, which was slick with blood, I hurried to the passenger door. He'd already opened it for me and was backing out of the alley before my butt hit the seat.

Slamming the door shut with my good hand, I fastened my seat belt and tried to remember how to breathe.

"Where did you get a car so fast?" I asked as we zoomed down the streets of New York so quickly the city flew by in smears of neon lights.

"I stole it."

I slumped in my seat with a smile of grim humor. I'd gone from courtesan college girl to a starring role in a real life rendition of Grand Theft Auto. All that was missing were the cops.

Kristos pulled out a cell phone and dialed with quick efficiency. In a clipped voice, he said, "I need a sweep of the penthouse and a clean-up crew at the restaurant. No humans on this one, I want kin we can trust." Not interested in a long conversation, he hung up abruptly.

"You think someone set you up?" I asked, horrified.

He shrugged. "Maybe."

"But why?"

He gave me a 'you should know the answer to that' look. "I'm rich. I'm powerful. I have enemies."

"If they wanted you, why would they keep shooting at me?"

"Because it might hurt me." He grimaced. "I should not have left you like that, but I really did think they would stop shooting once I was gone."

I frowned at him, trying to understand a world where hurting me was just a means to an end. We rolled to a stop at a red light and Kristos turned in his seat to face me. Apparently he didn't like what he saw, because he uttered a soft expletive and began taking off his shirt.

"You're hurt."

"Well, yeah, bullets will do that," I said, the stress of the evening's events making me flippant.

"Take this." He tossed his shirt to me, the muscles of his now bare torso flexing smoothly as he did so.

"And do what?" I fingered the fabric and inhaled the scent of him clinging to it. He smelled like cologne and wine and there was a smoky undertone that reminded me of a cigar.

"Staunch the blood."

"I'm not bleeding that much," I said.

"I won't take no for an answer. You're white as a ghost.

You need to stop the bleeding." He forced the shirt into my hand and then pressed it onto my shoulder.

I rolled my eyes, but obediently dabbed my shoulder with his shirt. More blood than I realized stained the white fabric. Maybe Kristos had been right. *Maybe you're going into shock,* a small voice said in my head. I told it to shut-up and applied pressure to my shoulder.

When blood trickled down my face and into my mouth, I just giggled. Kristos should be drinking it, not me.

"What's so funny?" Kristos asked.

I didn't respond because my breathing was too fast and yet I couldn't get enough air.

He gave me a quick glance and started when he saw me. "Oh, your face. Myra, I am so sorry. We'll get a doctor just as soon as we're someplace safe." He put a hand on my neck and pushed me down. "Lean forward and put your head between your knees. That should help with the breathing at least."

I did as he requested, staying like that the rest of the drive. There was another rush of blood from the cuts on my head, but then it slowed down. The position made my world small and dark. I could pretend I was safe and my labored breathing eased somewhat.

A few minutes later, Kristos stopped the car and turned off the engine. "We're here. Can you walk to the elevator?"

I sat up, blinking as all the blood that had pooled in my head rushed out of my brain. Another gush of blood dripped down the side of my face and stained my chest. I wiped away what I could and took in our surroundings. We were in an underground garage, parked in the spot right next to the elevator. A small security detail waited for us. I could tell they were with us and not against us because they waved to Kristos and he waved back.

"I can walk." That was probably a lie, but it sounded good. I'd come this far, that had to mean I was tough, right?

He gave a curt nod and got out of the car, nodding to the guards that came forward to meet him. I opened my door and hoisted myself out of the seat as two guards moved to escort me, hands on their guns, eyes scanning the parking garage for threats. Up until the last hour of my life, dating a guy with his own security would've been weird. Now I was grateful. The more guns on my side the better.

I wobbled to my feet. My body was too heavy and too light at the same time. My head floated for the moon, spinning like a Frisbee as it went, while my legs had morphed into leaden anchors. Leaning against the car, I slid my way toward the bumper, shutting the door behind me with a clumsy shove of my good hand.

When it came time for me to take my first step unsupported by the car, I crumpled. The pavement rushed up to meet me as my arms flailed, trying to help me balance. Before I could hit the ground, Kristos was there, strong arms cushioning my fall and bringing me up in a tight hold against his naked chest.

He carried me to the elevator and propped me up against the wall as he inserted a key into the control panel. The doors opened and we stepped inside. Security formed a line in front of the elevator, but didn't join us. Kristos pushed a button, visibly relaxing when the elevator began its ascent.

"Are you okay, Myra?" He took the shirt from my shoulder and dabbed my forehead.

"I'll live," I said, after a brief debate over the correct response to that question. I was a virgin trying to act the part of experienced call girl. I'd flashed an entire restaurant, been bitten by a vampire and involved in a shooting. Despite it all, I was pretty sure I would not die.

Amazing.

"Next time, wait for me to open the car door for you."

"Okay," I said, agreeably.

"You're starting to fall." Kristos reached over to pull me upright and close to him. I leaned against him as the elevator hummed around us. He had the strength of an immovable rock which I found reassuring just then.

I ran a hand over his chest, amazed at how smooth and firm he was. The guy worked out and I was almost grateful for my wounds because they had made him take off his shirt. The view was amazing. "Hey, Kristos?"

His arms tightened around me and he looked down at me, concern shining in his crystalline eyes. "Yes, Myra?"

"Is there going to be a next time with," I waved my hand in the air, "you know, *bullets*?"

"Not if I can help it."

I went back to touching his chest because repeating the same looping whorl on his skin kept me from losing my mind. I needed my world to be small, like when I'd had my head between my knees. Touching Kristos kept me from thinking about bullets and blood. "Your security sucks, by the way."

His jaw clenched. "I noticed."

"And you're hot," I added, deciding it needed to be said. His chest was especially magnificent. I wanted to say as much, but any further opportunity for discussion was lost as a deep blackness claimed me.

3

I woke with a start as someone dropped a frosty ice cube on my chest. For a moment, I couldn't remember what had happened, but then I saw Kristos standing in the doorway, a concerned look on his face, and it all came back to me. I lifted my head up, wincing as the pain from my injuries hit my nervous system.

Damn. That had been one hell of a night. To think my biggest fear had been having sex with a vampire. It just goes to show, you never know what will happen next, right? I fell back on my pillow, eyes finally registering the man holding a very cold stethoscope to my chest. He was middle-aged with a Ken-doll hair cut and brown eyes.

"What time is it?" I asked, my voice a hoarse croak.

"She needs some water," the man said to Kristos who nodded to someone behind him. The man smiled down at me. "Glad to see you awake. You slept all day and it's now just about ten p.m."

"Am I okay?" I checked my arms and legs. My shoulder was raw with small wounds, and, no doubt, my face wasn't much better.

"Lots of superficial abrasions on your shoulder and neck, but those will heal fairly quickly. You have a deep gash on your palm that I've stitched up and you have an IV to replace fluids." The man pointed to an IV bag hanging overhead, using the wooden bed post as an IV stand. "I'm Doctor Martin by the way."

"Myra Danson, but you probably knew that already. Thank you, doctor." I pushed myself into a sitting position and accepted the glass of water Kristos handed to me. I drank it in one long gulp, not even stopping to breathe, and gave him the empty glass. "Could I have some more?"

This time whomever Kristos was nodding to brought a pitcher and I drained it with greedy slurps; my throat was as dry as the Sahara. Dr. Martin checked my blood pressure and pulse while I drank.

"How is she, doctor?" Kristos asked.

"Her blood pressure has risen to normal levels, which is a good sign. Other than almost going into shock, her injuries are minor. I would recommend she take it easy tonight and keep the IV in. I'll take it out tomorrow and then she can just slowly return to normal activity from there."

"Will there be any scarring?" Kristos' gaze scanned my injuries, lingering on my face.

I paused mid-gulp at that. I hadn't even thought of scarring. Unbidden, the memory of Madame Rouge noting how my skin was unmarked rose in my mind. I wasn't particularly vain, but I had no desire to be maimed for life either.

"Maybe some minor discoloration. It just depends on her skin. If you are concerned about it, I would consult with a dermatologist. I can recommend someone if you like," the doctor said.

"I think that would be a good idea. Just leave the information with Orion on your way out," Kristos said.

The doctor nodded and turned to me. "I'll be back later to check on you. Rest as much as you can, alright?"

I smiled and nodded. "Sure. Thanks."

The doctor left and Kristos and I just stared at each other. He looked fit and trim, I noted. I had gotten the worst of last night's adventures, but I was alive, and...*not wearing my dress*. The realization dawned on me that someone had removed my dress and put me in a white undershirt.

I plucked at the v-neck t-shirt and looked anywhere but at Kristos. "Did you um..."

"Take off your dress?"

I nodded, staring very intently at a loose thread in the blue comforter on my bed.

"And see you naked?" There was a teasing note in his voice that told me he found my modesty funny. "Yes, and the view was stunning."

I bit my lip.

His tone became more serious. "Myra, it was an emergency. I had no idea how extensive your injuries were and the dress was in the way. I didn't see anything I wasn't going to see anyway, right?" When I didn't answer, he pushed. "Right?"

"I guess," I said. "How's the dress?"

"Dirty, but otherwise intact. I sent it out to the cleaners."

"Thanks." I gave him a shy smile.

"Well, this is awkward," Kristos finally said.

"I thought pretty much all of it was awkward." I smiled as I spoke so he would know I was trying to be funny.

"I can see how you might think that, but, for me, almost getting a courtesan killed is a new low. I'm sorry." His expression was contrite.

I lifted a shoulder in a shrug. "It's not like you planned it, right?"

"No and you'll be happy to know I fired all the security guards from last night."

"Did you find the shooter?"

"We're following up some leads," he said. He broke eye contact and his expression became guarded. I'd touched on a sore spot and he clearly didn't want to talk about it. I didn't blame him either. We barely knew each other and it was his business. Beyond being a bystander in the line of fire, it was none of mine.

Taking the hint, I changed the subject. "I guess you're stuck with me for another day." I gestured to the IV.

His gaze settled back on me and he relaxed. "It's the least I can do after last night. Besides, Madame Rouge has given me very clear directions on my obligations to your health."

"What did she say?" I clutched the bedspread, wringing it with my hands. Was I in trouble?

He sighed and ran a hand through his dark hair. "She called me some names, tripled your price and generally ripped me a new one."

Over a call girl? "Why would she do that?"

"Because if bad things happen to you, bad things happen to her business."

That made sense. If any of this mess did. "I'll be out of your hair as soon as I can. I don't want to inconvenience you."

He arched an eyebrow at me. "Do you remember what you said to me last night? Just before you passed out?"

My cheeks burned as I nodded.

He sat next to me on the bed and took my hand in his. "I'd like to try a do-over."

"Even at triple the price?"

He planted a kiss on my shoulder. "When it comes to you, yes." At my shocked expression, he gave a soft laugh. "You have a distinct flavor that reminds me of someone I can't quite place. Until I remember, you are going to drive me crazy."

I swallowed as he ran a finger down my cheek and over my collarbone. His touch was gentle, but sure and left me wanting more.

"You're blushing again."

"I'm always blushing," I said.

"I like it."

I shook my head. "I don't get it. What's the big deal about me blushing? You and Madame Rouge have gone on and on like I'm the coolest mood ring in the world. What gives?"

He gave me an amused smile, the corners of his eyes crinkling in a most attractive way. "I hadn't thought of you as a mood ring. It's an interesting picture." At my sigh of frustration, he held up a hand. "Okay, here is your explanation. Blushing is very erotic for vampires. It's blood rushing under your skin and it's tantalizing."

"So last night when you bit me--"

"Your blush drove me to it." He traced a finger from one collarbone over to the other, his eyes fixed on my pulse. He leaned in and claimed my lips with his in a fierce kiss. I could feel the pent-up passion in him, the desire to pick me up and crush me to his chest, but he held back, containing himself. Although I sensed the tension in his arms at the effort.

I moaned deep in my throat and made a mewling noise when his tongue stroked mine. I ran my hand up the back of his neck into his hair, fisting my hands in it and arching my body against his chest. Oh, yeah, I was going to totally rock this courtesan thing once I had some first-hand experience.

He sucked my bottom lip into his mouth and an electric current hit all my erogenous zones at once. Kristos pulled back then, with an expression of regret. "We probably shouldn't go any further. You haven't even been conscious for an hour. This really isn't the time."

I tucked my hair behind my ear and tried to remember how to breathe. Damn, I knew he was right, but I didn't want him to stop. Desire pulsed through my body, and with Kristos breaking contact, it became an itch I couldn't scratch. It was frustrating. *Well, hello there sexual frustration, I don't believe we've met before.*

He stood up and kissed the top of my head. "I've asked one of my female staff to bring some clothes for you to wear for now. Madame Rouge has promised to send her team over with a wardrobe during the day. That will keep you busy until you're well enough to do everything I want to do with you."

I cleared my throat. "I just hope there's underwear this time."

He laughed. "After everything that happened last night, the underwear is what you worry about?"

"In case you haven't noticed, I'm not much for flashing. It wasn't even on my bucket list." I smiled at him. "My life goal at this point is to wear underwear at all times."

"Surely not all the time?" He leveled a gaze at me so scorching my skin felt hot even though he hadn't touched me.

I squirmed, the heat of embarrassment flushing my cheeks. I cleared my throat and clarified, "At all times in public."

"I'll see that you have some. I wouldn't want this to stress you out or anything." He was grinning at me, thoroughly enjoying my discomfiture. "I have some business to attend to before the sun rises. We'll talk tomorrow night. Make yourself at home. Rest, eat, figure out your panty problem."

4

After Kristos left, I slept for a bit, waking when someone came into my room. I bolted upright and relaxed when I saw it was just a woman with some clothes for me. She had a muscular, wiry frame and short blonde hair with dark eyes. The expression on her face was one of distaste or unhappiness. I did not get a good vibe from her.

She looked me up and down and gave me one of those fake smiles girls give the competition. "Kristos asked me to bring you something to wear. Although I don't know why." She dumped a pile of folded clothes on the bed and moved to leave.

"Wait, what do you mean by that?" I asked.

She paused as if thinking about her response. "He likes his girls naked. I'm surprised he even let you wear one of his shirts." Her tone was accusatory.

"I had nothing to do with it," I said feeling the need to defend myself. "I was unconscious. He put it on for me."

She pursed her lips and raised her eyebrows. "Lucky you.

He's not usually that sentimental."

"I'm Myra, by the way." I gave her a bright smile to show there were no hard feelings. Her attitude bothered me, but maybe we could work past it to some semblance of friendliness.

She shrugged. "Who cares? You're just the flavor of the moment. Enjoy your T-shirt, while you can." With that, she turned on her heel and left.

Flummoxed, I gaped as she went. When I recovered my composure, I pulled on the yoga pants she'd brought, but kept Kristos' shirt. It smelled like him and I liked it. Barefoot, with my IV bag held high in one hand, I padded through what turned out to be a penthouse suite on the top floor of an apartment building. A clock by the front door showed the time as four a.m. It was still night, but barely.

The large suite had an open floor plan in the common areas. Floor to ceiling windows showed the skyline of New York to its full effect and drove home how much money Kristos must have to pay for such a view. The furniture was sparse and Scandinavian in design. There was some art, mostly abstract, but a few paintings made me shudder, featuring women bound and whipped until they were bloody. Not my thing so I moved on, refusing to dwell on it. One person's art is another person's trash.

In the generous aisle kitchen, I made a meal out of fresh fruit, yogurt and orange juice. It was early, but I was hungry and off schedule. The last time I'd eaten had been at the restaurant. I ate at the counter, nodding as a uniformed guard passed by on what

I assumed was his patrol. He ignored me and I wondered if he knew I was just the flavor of the moment too?

5

The next morning, Jacques and Savon came into my room like a breeze of fresh air. I'd rested as much as I could, had the joy of navigating the bathroom while attached to an IV, called my mom to check in and raided the fridge three times. Recuperation was boring and I needed a distraction.

"Hello, umm, what's your name again?" Jacques asked as he heaved a very large suitcase onto my bed.

"Myra," I said, my body bouncing up as the weight of the suitcase shook the entire bed.

"Oh right. So how was getting shot?" He dropped a garment bag on top of the suitcase and unzipped it in one smooth movement.

"Scary."

"But very rewarding," he said over his shoulder as he headed for the closet, a stack of swirling fabric in his hands. "You are making bank off this, honey." Hangers clanged as he hung the clothes.

"Really?" I was a little fuzzy on payment details. We'd long surpassed the original fee I'd been quoted, both on time and events. The only thing that gave me pause was we hadn't had sex and Kristos hadn't done more than sample my blood. Technically, I'd done nothing in my job description.

"Madame Rouge makes the vamps pay if the girl gets hurt. Plus Kristos commissioned a full wardrobe for you." He pulled a gorgeous red satin gown out of the garment bag with a flourish. "That only happens when he likes you. If Kristos likes you, you're making good money."

"Have a lot of girls been shot?" I asked, nervous. I knew what Madam Rouge had said about rough sex, but were shootings a regular thing?

Savon shook his head as he sorted through his make-up case. "There's never been a shooting. Sometimes a vamp gets a little rough maybe, but they lose their membership for that so our client list is pretty safe."

"Are you ready to see your new wardrobe?" Jacques asked.

I nodded and watched as he paraded at least a dozen evening gowns around the room. They came in a rainbow of silken hues and were all pretty much designed for wardrobe malfunctions.

I shuddered remembering my last one. "Is there any underwear?"

"Yes, Kristos requested some for you. Why, I don't know." Jacques tossed a plastic shopping bag to me.

I opened it to find a bunch of tangled lace. I teased out one piece from the jumble and found it was a sheer lace thong. More sorting and I found a matching bra. There were five sets of the same design, just different colors and all see-through.

I really missed my mass produced undies. "What do vampires have against underwear?"

"Why do they drink blood?" Savon countered.

I frowned at the question. "Because they need it to live? It's their food?"

"Then why tie it to sex?" he asked.

I had no idea and just shook my head.

"Didn't Madame Rouge explain any of this to you?" Jacques sounded annoyed.

I raised my eyebrows. "There's an explanation?"

Savon nodded. "Yes. Sex enhances the flavor of blood, fills it with endorphins and other feel good hormones. It's like getting buzzed on fine wine. So vampires are very sex oriented and clothing sometimes annoys them."

Jacques sniffed. "Some like to add pain into the mix too." There was a guarded look in his eyes that said he knew more about that than he cared to admit. He took more dresses from the garment bag and whirled away from me to hang them up in the closet.

I blanched remembering the strangely violent pictures in the apartment. "You mean, like whipping?"

"Yeah, but don't worry, Madame Rouge wouldn't contract you out for that without training," Savon said. He opened the large cosmetic case he'd brought with him and rummaged through it, setting piles of make-up on the bed.

"Training? You mean, I would practice being whipped first?" I blinked, taken aback by the idea.

"Pretty much," said Jacques.

I looked at them with wide eyes and Savon gave a 'vampires will be vampires' shrug.

Unable to picture how someone learns to be whipped and quite uncomfortable with the idea, I changed the subject. "Do you guys know Kristos well?"

"We know of him," Savon said, still sorting through his case. "Sometimes we take his calls when Madame is busy."

"What's he like?"

"The girls love him. He's left a string of broken hearts for Madame Rouge to put back together. Be careful he doesn't do the same to you," Savon said. "Now, here is your make-up. I will show you how to use it all before I go." He shoved a pile of lipstick, liner and eye shadow toward me.

"Thanks, Savon."

He smiled, and began to say something, but Jacques interrupted him. Unzipping the suitcase with a flourish, he said, "Are you ready for your day wardrobe?"

Not waiting for a response, he opened the suitcase and began tossing clothes all over the bed. "I have jeans, designer of course, and several different tops depending on if you want to dress up or dress down."

I picked up a pair of jeans. The label was not a name I'd

heard before, but it was clearly expensive. I had a hard time understanding why denim had to be designer, but Jacques had a budget that could probably buy a new car every week while I still shopped at Target.

Noticing my lack of reaction, Jacques gave a little huff of irritation. "Go put them on, oh ye of little faith."

I just looked at him, taken aback. "What?"

"You won't understand until you put them on." He made a shooing motion. "Go. Enter the temple of high fashion and be enlightened."

I wanted to roll my eyes, but kept my emotions in check. If Jacques and I ever started competing on attitude, I was in for a world of hurt. Swinging my legs over the side of the bed, I grabbed the pants, snagged a pair of lace underwear and took them into the bathroom. Ditching my yoga pants, I pulled on the underwear followed by the jeans. They fit perfectly.

"Go out to the entry way, there's a full length mirror there," Jacques called through the bathroom door.

With a shrug, I did as he requested. The mirror showed me the power of designer jeans. My legs were long and lithe and my ass had been lifted into a perfect rounded mound.

I couldn't stop myself from strutting a bit as I went back to my room. "Wow," I said.

Jacques just nodded and passed me a shirt. "Here, put something on besides that ghastly white shirt. It does nothing for you."

I accepted the blue off-the-shoulder tunic top with a frown. Holding up my arm, I pointed to the IV. "What does the fashion handbook say about getting dressed with this thing?"

"If you need it, you need it, but the bag is empty," Savon said with a pointed look to Jacques.

"You think I should take it out for her?" he asked Savon.

"You can take it out?" I was giddy at the thought of getting rid of my medical ball and chain.

"Oh all right," Jacques said with an aggravated sigh. He strode over to me and ripped the tape holding the IV in place off in one swift movement.

I screeched in pain and jumped back, but he gripped my wrist and held me in place. "Don't move unless you want to bleed all over your very expensive clothes."

I went still and closed my eyes as he teased out the IV and grabbed a tissue from the nightstand to press on the wound.

He took my other hand and placed it on the tissue and then bent my elbow up. "There, all set."

I opened my eyes and blinked. "How do you know how to do that?"

He shrugged. "Life experience."

"Too much time with vampires?" I asked.

Jacques rolled his eyes at me and gave a little sigh of exasperation. "None of your beeswax."

I winced at the rebuke. I'd obviously hit a sore spot. Why did we have so much friction? I didn't get it. Hiding my embarrassment, I lifted the tissue to check my arm and since it didn't seem to be bleeding, I went back into the bathroom to change. I put on a bra and then pulled on the tunic. Its lightweight fabric settled on my shoulders like a cloud and the white embroidery around the neckline gave the top a Moroccan flair. Back in the bedroom, I stashed Kristos' shirt under my pillow knowing, if Jacques got his hands on it, I would never see it again.

"The tops were all selected to showcase your neck and chest," Jacques explained, all business now. "Part of your job is to highlight your assets and be presentable at all times."

"Got it," I said, relieved to be moving on to safer topics.

He didn't respond other than to fasten a braided brown leather belt around my waist. Then, digging through the suitcase, he produced a pair of blue pumps, with matching embroidery.

Inwardly I groaned. More heels. Great. To Jacques, I simply said, "Thank you." At least I wasn't wearing a dress.

Jacques stood back and looked me over with a critical eye. I struck a few poses, doing my best to channel my inner model. "You'll do, I guess," he said finally, his approval lackluster.

I opened my mouth to say something, my irritation with the man running high, but Savon intervened, saying smoothly, "Jacques, you know what we need? Something to drink. Since you know the layout here, can you get us something? I'm parched."

I expected Jacques to resist the request; he didn't strike me as the type to fetch someone a drink. To my surprise, though, Jacque gave a curt nod and whipped around on the heel of his cowboy boot, off to the kitchen. From his body language it seemed like maybe he was glad to have an excuse to get away from me.

I watched him go with a puzzled frown. Such a prickly pear. "Did I do something wrong?"

"Sometimes you can't do anything right with him, at which point I try to distract him with something else," Savon said, his tone matter-of-fact. He pulled more stuff from his case. "I also brought you some hair products. Oh, and a toothbrush, I figured you would need one."

I accepted the bundle of hair gels and oral hygiene implements he handed to me. "Thanks, I appreciate your help."

Somewhere in the apartment, glass crashed to the ground and both Savon and I froze.

"Jacques," he whispered, rushing out the door.

I followed and we found Jacques in the grand foyer by the front door. He was on his knees in front of the double doors that offset the entrance to the apartment. Shards of glass gleamed in a puddle of water on the marble floor. The doors had been closed all day, but now stood open and it was impossible not to notice the contents of the room beyond. Whips hung on the walls. Chains dangled from the ceiling and in the center of the room sat a bed draped in red velvet. There were other things I didn't understand. Sawhorses. Wooden pieces of furniture whose purpose was a mystery to me. Again the art from the apartment haunted me, poking at my subconscious with a warning whisper.

"Are you okay?" I knelt down next to Jacques and began to

gingerly collect glass in my good hand, the one that hadn't been sliced open the night before. Here I was again dealing with broken glass and a strong sense of *déjà vu* prickled up my spine. I shook it off and focused on Jacques, who was determinedly not looking into the torture chamber, his gaze fixed on the small area of carpet in front of him.

"Jacques?" I asked, trying to break through his shield of silence.

He looked up at me then and tears glimmered in his eyes. "I had to see if it was still there."

"Sorry?"

"I used to do what you do. I used to be a courtesan." He nodded toward the room. "And they broke me."

Savon kneeled next to Jacques and patted him on the back. "Jacques, this is not good for you." He stood up and pulled Jacques with him by the hand. "Myra, do you mind cleaning up? I'm going to get him out of here before he has a complete breakdown."

I nodded. "Yeah sure. Is he okay?"

Savon flashed a smile at me that was meant to be reassuring, only it didn't reach his eyes. "Yes, of course. Sometimes his past is a little more present than he can take."

"I thought I would be okay," Jacques said in a soft murmur, looking at Savon with wide eyes. "It's all different now."

"Yes it is, but you are still the same." Savon led Jacques down the hall. "Now come, let's get our bags and go." They disappeared into my room and I resumed picking up shards of glass with cautious fingers.

What had happened to Jacques? Why would he say they broke him? And why did Kristos have an elaborate torture chamber in his apartment? The last question bothered me the most.

When they emerged from my room, bags in hand, I stood up and walked with them to the door.

"Savon?"

He turned, just about to step out of the apartment. "Yes?"

I shot a nervous glance at Jacques who moved like a robot set on autopilot. He stared straight ahead with a fixed gaze, body posture rigid as if trying to keep himself together through sheer will. I didn't want to upset him, but I needed to know. "Am I really safe here?" That room was made to tie somebody up and beat them bloody. For all I knew, that somebody was me.

Savon caught my look to Jacques and nodded. "Yes. This is all old history. Vampires share space a lot. Now this place is Kristos' but a--"

"Monster," Jacques finished for him, his voice flat.

"Another vampire used to live here." Savon laid a comforting hand on Jacques arm. "But he's gone now and he can't hurt anyone." To me, he said, "You'll be fine."

I nodded. "Okay. Thanks for your help."

They left and the silent security guard shut the door after them. I continued on to the kitchen where I disposed of the glass I'd been holding in my hand and tried not to think of monsters.

6

Around dusk, another security guard escorted Doctor Martin into my room. He smiled at me warmly. "How are you feeling, Miss Danson?"

"Myra, please. I'm good." I held up my hand and showed him the IV was gone. When he frowned, I hastened to explain, "The bag was empty and I didn't know when you were coming."

He nodded and opened his briefcase. "All right. Well, let me check your blood pressure and just make sure you aren't running low. Being around vampires, you want to keep up your blood volume." He pulled out a cuff and stethoscope.

I held my arm out and remained still while he inflated the cuff until it felt like it would amputate my arm. He listened for a moment and then let go of the bulb.

The cuff hissed as it deflated. "Your blood pressure is perfect and you don't seem to be dehydrated. I think we can declare you cured. Just be sure to drink lots of fluids to replace what you've lost." He patted me on the shoulder. "I need to see you late next week so I can remove those stitches in your hand, all right?"

"Sure. Do you come to me or do I come to you?"

"Kristos will let me know."

"Yes I will," said Kristos stepping into the room. He flashed a smoldering smile my way and I, predictably, blushed. "Thank you, doctor, you can go now."

Doctor Martin nodded and gathered his things. "I'll be in touch."

"Thanks," I said as he left the room. Turning my attention to Kristos, I said, "Hi."

"You're looking better." He came to sit next to me on the bed and took my hand in his.

I gave his hand a little squeeze, happy to see him. "Yes, thank you."

"Nice outfit." He ran a finger along the collar, making me shiver. "Ready for dinner?"

I shrugged. "Sure. What did you have in mind? More gun fights at swanky restaurants?" I put a hand to my mouth surprised by my sarcastic response, but Kristos just chuckled.

"Very funny. I have something better in mind." He pulled my hand away and kissed me.

Pushing him back, I said, "Wait a second. We need to talk." I took his hand and tugged him toward the hallway. "Come on."

Kristos allowed me to lead him to the torture chamber Jacques had uncovered earlier. "What is this room?" Now that I stood inside, it seemed even worse. Everywhere I looked, there was a whip or some kind of shackle. The room was a prison without prisoners, a place where you lost your freedom.

Kristos looked abashed. If he'd had any circulation, he would have blushed. "It's a predilection of my kind."

"What? Torture?" Fear shot through me. "Were you...were you going to *beat* me?"

His gaze steady, he said, "Not any time soon. It's something you work up to and it's not for everyone."

I edged toward the door, heart in my throat. What had I gotten myself into? Sex and blood were one thing, whips and chains something else entirely.

Seeing my panic, Kristos held his hands up and open as if to show he was harmless. "Myra, this is nothing to be afraid of."

I continued to edge away from him and the room until I stood on the threshold. Kristos followed me, matching my slow pace, his blue eyes locked with mine.

"Have I acted without honor at any time since we've met?" He asked, his gaze hardening.

I shook my head. "No." Quite the opposite in fact.

"That is not about to change. Now come, I am sure you have questions and I would prefer to answer them elsewhere." He held out a hand.

For a long moment I hesitated, but then remembering my mother, I took it. Kristos hadn't hurt me. He'd been nothing but kind and there was no reason for me to run screaming, even if his home was equipped for the Inquisition.

He led me out of the room, shutting the doors after us and escorted me to the dining room. Candles gleamed in the center of the table, highlighting a vase of red roses and a plate heaped with what appeared to be roast chicken and mashed potatoes. A bottle of wine waited in a silver ice bucket. Despite my frequent raids on his fridge, my stomach growled.

He smiled at the sound. "Are you always hungry or do you just never eat?"

"Since I eat, I guess the answer is I'm always hungry." I slid into the chair as he pulled it out for me. "At least tonight, I have underwear."

"I'm not sure that's an improvement." He settled into his seat where the setting consisted only of a wine glass. Pouring the wine, he said, "Underwear makes it difficult to top your entrance last night."

"You may enjoy my humiliation, but I don't." I sipped my wine, relishing its fruity tang.

He paused, glass halfway to his mouth. "You misunderstand. Women have thrown themselves at me in a predictable fashion for centuries to the point where it's dull. You were different and I like new things."

"Is that how you picked up your little torture hobby?" I immediately wanted to take the words back. Kristos was a client, someone I needed to impress, not snark on. What was with all the flippant comments? *Get a grip Myra*, I ordered myself. *Mind your manners.*

His jaw clenched and his expression grew stern. "First, this is not my private home. It's owned by my company and is used by multiple people. It's furnished to satisfy more than just my needs. Second, you have no idea how good a whip can feel. Third, other than an open mind, I will never require something from you that you aren't willing to give."

I bit my lip and focused on my plate, the aroma of perfectly roasted chicken suddenly failing to entice my appetite. He was mad and it was my fault. "I'm sorry. It's just one of Madame Rouge's people had a bad experience there."

"You aren't them and I am not Ivan."

"Ivan?" I furrowed my brow, unfamiliar with the name.

"One of my associates. He's no longer with the company." He shifted in his seat, reaching for the wine bottle to top off our glasses. "Let's change the subject. I understand you're in college. What major?"

"Business." Although the world of textbooks and professors felt like it was a different dimension given my current circumstances.

That made him smile. "You want to be a CEO when you grow up?"

I shook my head and cut up my chicken. "No. I'm more interested in entrepreneurship and small start-ups."

He cocked his head and raised an eyebrow, curious. "Ah, you have a business idea?"

"A few," I hedged. My appetite resurfaced and I began to eat. The succulent chicken and gravy filled me with the warmth of comfort food.

He smiled at me over his wine glass. "You're smart to be careful with your intellectual property."

"Thanks. Speaking of business, what does your company do?"

"I'm the CEO of a conglomerate with interests in medicine and renewable energy sources. One thing vampires excel at is innovation over the long term."

"So you'll be CEO forever?"

He watched as I drank my wine, eyes focused on the movement of my throat. "No, we cycle through to keep things looking human. I'll be CEO for a few decades and then someone else comes in to be the public figurehead."

"Why do you want to look human? Doesn't everyone know you're a vampire already?"

He shrugged. "We have survived by our discretion and old habits die hard. We've only been integrating openly into society for the last few decades. One step at a time."

"Not to mention I could see competitors claiming unfair advantage." I paused, struck by a thought. "There are human CEOs right? The corporate world isn't run by an oligarchy of vampires is it?" If true, it would completely change how I read the business case studies in my textbooks.

He laughed. "No. We aren't that proliferate."

"Can I ask you a more personal question?" I wanted to address some of the concerns I had about blood courtesans.

Kristos crossed his arms and leaned back in his chair. "I can't promise to answer."

"That's fair. Okay, here's the thing, you're attractive, you're rich, what do you need to pay me for? Can't you just get a girlfriend or something?"

"That's an easy one. Would you want to be married to every meal you ate?" He pointed to my plate. "You can eat and the meal is done. A girlfriend is a meal that nags and demands attention. Worse, it's like agreeing to eat only bananas for the rest of my life."

"You have a point, but no girlfriends, ever?" That puzzled me. Did vampires not fall in love?

He waved a hand. "Every so often I have had a relationship. We are not immune to the laws of attraction, but it's difficult to date a human."

"Yeah, what do you do when you're sick of bananas?"

"Hire another courtesan." He shifted in his seat. "Sex and feeding are so entwined for us that it's just easier to keep it at a business level. Otherwise, we are forever cheating on our significant others and," he waved a hand, "then it's just too much drama."

"What about other vampires?"

"Yes, it happens. Not so much for me. I find female vampires to be overly aggressive. They gain so much strength, they lose the vulnerability that I find attractive. Vampires are all hard edges and I like soft curves." He reached over and ran a finger along my forearm, the simple touch causing me to flush.

"That's an insightful comment coming from a guy." I picked up my knife as an excuse to break contact and cut another piece of chicken.

"I've had a lot of time to think about these things." He watched me with an amused gleam as if he knew how nervous he made me. "So what about you?"

"What about me?" I asked, confused.

"Your boyfriends."

"Oh. None." Realizing that wasn't an answer that would jive with my employment application, I hastened to add, "None to worry about."

"Any long term relationships?"

His gaze probed mine and I tried to look nonchalant. "Oh sure." If you counted crushes from afar. I'd spent about a year in unrequited lust for a guy in high school. It never went anywhere because I was a debate team geek complete with braces. In college the braces had come off, but mom's chemo started taking up more than my spare time. I'd barely noticed anything except how far behind I was in my classes.

"Come here." He held out a hand, waiting while I put down my silverware and set aside my napkin. Standing, I let him pull me onto his lap, straddling his legs with mine. "By the time I am done with you, I will know all your secrets, carnal or otherwise." He kissed the spot on my neck where my pulse jumped, pressing his tongue against it. An electric arousal shivered through me and I gasped when his hand grazed my nipple, causing it to harden.

Cradling my head, he kissed his way up my neck to my lips. I moaned at the increasing sexual tension. Between his legs, a hard bulge pushed against the softness of my thighs.

He pulled away, hands settling on my hips. "Doctor Martin has made me promise not to feed tonight, but I do plan on a sip as well as other wickedness. Is that acceptable to you?"

I nodded as nerves swirled in my stomach threatening to overthrow my meal. Finding my voice, I said, "Kristos?"

"Yes?"

"I need to tell you something." I stared down at my hands, wringing them with anxiety because I knew what came next and feared it. I suddenly lost faith in myself. What had I been thinking? Pretending I knew anything at all about sex was a special kind of lunacy. The lie felt wrong. *I* felt wrong. He deserved to know the truth and I wanted to stop making up a past that didn't exist.

"I can see something is bothering you." He took my hands in his secure grip and gave me a reassuring squeeze. "Try not to worry, I know what it's like to be a new courtesan and I will be very gentle with you."

"It's not that," I said. "Or, it's not *just* that."

"What is it then? Are you menstruating? We can work around that you know."

I shook my head. "I'm a virgin." Worrying my lip, I waited

for his response.

He was silent for a moment, then, "Really?"

There was a delight I didn't understand in his voice and I risked a look at his face. He was smiling and appeared to be very pleased.

He gave a little tug of my hands, trying to capture my attention. "What an unexpected surprise."

My eyes downcast, I said, "I thought you would be mad."

He frowned. "Why?"

"Because Madame Rouge made it sound like virgins were bad."

He waved a dismissive hand. "For her, maybe, but not for me." And then he was kissing me, hungrily claiming my lips, his hands massaging their way up my spine to the back of my neck. Deepening the kiss, he gripped the hem of my shirt and broke contact to lift it over my head. Tossing it aside, he bent down and kissed the top of each breast, tongue slipping under the fabric of my bra to tease my nipples. The sensation was so intense, I had to hold onto his shoulders to keep myself upright. A hunger I'd never fed, came alive and full of craving.

"It's okay then?" I frowned, not trusting his quick acceptance.

"More than okay," Kristos said. "Unless you want to stop?" He went still and looked at me.

I shook my head. "No, I don't want to stop."

"What do you want?" His gaze searched mine and I had

that feeling again of being in a freefall.

"You," I whispered utterly charmed by this debonair vampire and his easy way with my body that quickened me with desire. "I want you to be my first."

"Good. I want to be your first too." He unhooked my bra then and peeled it off me, smiling wolfishly as my breasts came into view. Hefting one globe in each hand, thumbs caressing the tips, he said, "I can hear your heart. It beats faster when I touch you."

Caught up in the effect of his touch, I had no response other than a hitch in my breathing.

"Tell me, has any man made you feel this way?"

I shook my head.

"Just me?"

I nodded.

"Say the words, Myra." He then tugged my hair until I lifted my chin up, exposing my throat which he covered with kisses.

"Just you," I gasped.

At that, he leaned down to suck a nipple while continuing to play with the other, his tongue stroked me with a light, feathery touch. Then the pressure increased as he suckled the tip, which stiffened in response. When he flicked his tongue across my nipple, I moaned and arched my back, pushing my breasts into his face. The sensation in my breast bordered on pain without leaving pleasure. The feeling left me unsatisfied and wanting more.

He released me with a laugh. "And you think you don't like whippings."

Confused, I looked at him. "What?"

"That, my dear, was a thorough tongue lashing." He moved to my other breast, taking the nipple and areola in his mouth with a hard suck. The bristles of his facial hair scraped my tender skin and his tongue showed me no mercy. As before, he stroked me until my nipple hardened into a nub and then he whipped his tongue across it, in hard, short strokes. My first whipping and it felt so good.

My hips spun in small circles and I threw my head back with a heavy sigh. My fingers had gone numb from holding onto him so tightly.

"I think it's time to retire to the bedroom, don't you?"

I nodded and then on impulse, reached down to kiss him, tentatively parting his lips for a French kiss. He tasted like salt and wine. His fangs were sharp as razor blades, threatening to nick my tongue with every pass. I came up for air. "Thank you."

"For what?"

"For being so kind."

"Kind enough to almost get you killed." There was a hint of bitterness in his voice.

I shrugged. "Kind enough to take care of me. To put up with all my bumbling mistakes and lies."

"Are you saying we're even?"

"Yeah, I think so." I went to kiss him again, finding I

craved his touch. He met me half-way and took control of my mouth as he stood up. Cradling me in his arms, he swept me out of the dining room and down the hall.

7

Dark wood panels lined the walls of Kristos' bedroom. The hint of red in the cherry wood stain was the only color as everything else was black from the duvet to the carpet. Kristos set me down on the bed and tugged at the waistband of my jeans until the button came undone. He eased them past my hips, peeling them off and tossing them onto the floor. With a smoldering expression, he hooked his thumbs around my underwear and took those off as well. I was now naked with nothing to hide behind.

"Your skin is amazing. Like porcelain." He traced a finger over my collarbone. "And then you blush." His finger ran between my breasts. I looked down to see a red flush creeping over my sternum.

"I always hated how much I blushed," I said, breathless.

"And now?"

"You're convincing me of its charm. Bit by bit." I smiled up at him, drinking in his dark good looks, giddy with the idea of what would come next. I was going to lose my virginity to a vampire and the idea no longer scared me. Quite the opposite in fact, I found it titillating now that I knew the fire he could ignite in my senses.

He moved to take off his shirt, but I held up a hand. "Wait. Let me." I stood and took over, pushing the small buttons of his dress shirt through their holes. His muscles flexed whenever my fingers brushed against his skin. I eased the shirt down his shoulders, pausing to kiss his chest and inhale his scent.

With a grin, I sucked his bottom lip into my mouth, nibbling until he groaned, hands going to caress my breasts. I rubbed my nipples across his chest, delighting in the sensation of his smooth skin on my aching tips.

"You're an adventurous virgin." His tone was amused.

I gave a shy smile. "You bring it out in me." Not waiting for a response, I kissed my way down his neck to his chest. Slowly kneeling, I planted my lips on his stomach and then tugged his belt free. Unfastening his pants, I let them fall to the floor, waiting for him to step out of them and kick them away before removing his boxers.

His underwear gave me pause. It was the point of no return and I found myself nervous. What we were about to do marked a huge personal transition and I lingered on the threshold, fingers barely touching his waistband.

Sensing the shift in my emotions, Kristos put his hands lightly over mine and together we took off his boxers. His cock sprang to attention the second it was free. It was long and large and

I both feared and craved it.

"Don't worry, Myra. It will fit."

I bit my lip, embarrassed by my innocence.

Kristos pulled me to my feet. "Are you okay?"

Eyes focused on the floor, I merely nodded.

"You seem upset. Is something wrong?" He lifted my chin with an insistent finger, gaze probing mine, full of concern.

"What if I'm not enough?"

"You are already more than I could hope for." He touched my throat and then leaned down to suck the skin of my neck into his mouth, rolling it with his lips. Pushing me back on the bed, he nuzzled my breasts in turn as his hand wandered to the nexus between my legs. "Spread your legs for me, love. Let me touch you."

I complied and he stroked my core with a gentle finger, making me shiver.

"Try not to worry. Just let go and trust me." He paused to look up at me, holding my gaze until I nodded under the weight of his attention. His eyes had a knack for making me feel as if the world was spinning while I stood still.

Kristos nuzzled my breast, lips closing softly over my nipple, his tongue probing and caressing it into a hard nub. Desire shot through my body as if my nipple was the 'power button' for my sexuality. Wetness gathered in my center, coating his hand, which had never stopped touching me.

He gave me a wide grin that told me my response was just

what he wanted and promised more. Turning his attentions to the other breast, he lashed the nipple into a stiff peak. Between my breasts and the stimulation of my overheated core, my hips began to circle as the energy of desire pooled between my legs with no place to go. The need for a release mounted and I looked at Kristos with wide, pleading eyes.

He chuckled. "You win."

"Win what?" I asked, my voice a breathy pant.

"The title of hottest virgin I've ever met." He ran one hand over my stomach, smiling as it trembled at the contact. "You're so ready and I've barely touched you."

I bit my lip, uncomfortable at the compliment.

"When you bite your lip like that, it makes me want to bite." He smiled wide, revealing fangs at the ready. Removing his hand from my core, he put a finger to my mouth, tugging my lip out from under my teeth. "Taste yourself." He pushed his finger into my mouth. With hesitant swipes of my tongue, I licked and a salty, musky flavor hit my taste buds. It was me, I realized. It was all my desire, all the pent-up need his touch had made tangible.

"Are you going to feed from me now?" I asked, suddenly tight with the wrong kind of tension. I was afraid of what I was about to do. Lost in unknown territory with a guide who could make me purr with his touch alone or rip my throat out with sharp, pointy teeth.

He pursed his lips and looked at me for a moment. "Not yet. For us, sex is like picking fruit. Green on the vine is bitter. I want you at your ripest, fullest moment." He kissed my shoulder and fondled my breast. "When you come for me, then I'll drink. Just a small taste, love. You'll hardly miss it."

Kristos pushed me back on the bed and then pulled my hips down to the edge of the mattress as he kneeled between my legs.

"Will it hurt?" I propped myself up on my elbows and looked down at him as his gaze focused on my wet center.

"No more than a sting, but you'll be way past feeling anything but pleasure." Hooking my knees over his arms, he spread my legs wide and covered my core with soft, fluttering kisses. Just as I became accustomed to that, his tongue parted my folds and flicked the sensitive nub there.

I gasped and arched off the bed.

"Everything all right?"

I lifted my head to see him watching me with an amused expression. "Yes," I managed to say breathlessly.

"I know the first time can be scary. Especially today. Americans are raised to believe in romance. I come from a time, Myra, when fucking the right man was everything and love had little value." He dipped his head between my legs again and wiggled his tongue up and down, making my thighs clench, grasping at nothing.

Despite the carnal distraction of his mouth, I asked, "When was that?"

"Ancient Rome." He paused to pull my clit into his mouth with gentle suction. My hands fisted in the sheets and my hips twisted in bigger and bigger circles, until he had to push them firmly back down to the bed. He lifted his head then, giving me a moment of respite. "What I'm saying is, you have chosen well and you are securing your family's future. There is great honor in that. There will be time for romance later. For now, let yourself go and trust me to take you where you need to go. Be glad you are giving yourself to the right man."

His tongue returned to my nether lips, pushing them apart to massage my sensitive nub. There was no stopping for conversation this time. I closed my eyes to better concentrate on the orgasm that swelled deep in my core, heavy and wet, ready to burst.

Again my hips bounced up, and again Kristos pinned me down in order to keep me where he wanted it. There was something so primal about that small act of restraint. I was not in control, the fate of my orgasm rested with him. He had all the power, and my only choice was to submit. Yet still I strained to take the pleasure faster, harder. I wanted release.

My body bucked and fought him, but he was so strong, all he had to do was merely tighten his grip. The legend of super human strength flashed through my mind. He certainly had super human speed, which made me think of how fast his tongue might go.

My breath heaved in short pants as the climax prepared to explode. With my hips pinned down so tightly, all I could do was arch my back, wishing his mouth was on my breasts too. The memory of my nipples hardening for him took me over the edge and I cried out. Big contractions of pleasure shook me followed by fluttering pulses. He never stopped lapping up my juices and then I realized, when still he didn't stop, that he was actually feeding.

I pushed myself up so I could see his throat convulse as he swallowed. I was stunned. I thought vampires fed from the neck. I had never expected such an intimate act would also include blood. Of course, I hadn't really known anything until this moment and what I did know about sex with vampires was still woefully inadequate.

To my surprise, another orgasm rose up, unbidden. I was turned on, I realized by watching him and the fact he was literally eating me. It made me feel powerful and incredibly sexy. While the second orgasm wasn't as strong as the first one, it still forced me to lay back and shudder in surrender. His tongue swept over my sensitive center, fueling the fire in my nervous system and almost crossing the line into pain.

Then he was standing, his cock impossibly large and aiming straight for me. My breathing hitched and panic flashed through me.

"Don't think, just feel," he said, his eyes swallowing up mine until I couldn't tell where I ended and he began. His cock wedged itself in the entrance to my wet passage and pushed, insisting on entry. "Try to relax and open for me." He nuzzled my neck and kissed his way down to my breast, teasing my nipple into hard prominence.

Very patiently and deliberately, he played with my breasts until my hips began to move under him. Ever so slowly, he inched his way inside, expanding my walls wide until they ached.

"You're so wet and tight. I can't wait to show you how good it's going to be." He eased out and then pumped into me with one fluid movement that made me hiss as pleasure and pain mixed. The sensation of my virginity tearing away made me bite my lip, a reaction that made Kristos' eyes burn with desire.

He claimed my lips in a bruising kiss, capturing my moans in his mouth as he took me in slow motion. Gradually, he picked up speed, going faster and faster until my breasts bounced with the force of his re-entry. I reached up and grabbed his shoulders. The stitches in my palm stretched in protest, but I ignored the minor discomfort in favor of holding on. I didn't know where the ride was going to take me and I feared it would shatter me into a million pieces.

Soon I was thrusting up to meet him, wishing I could take him deeper. My need was insatiable and he only satisfied it in glancing blows as his cock buried itself to the hilt inside me. I needed more.

As if sensing that, Kristos put my feet on his shoulders and took me with powerful thrusts of his hips. His entire body felt as hard as his cock; throbbing muscle bouncing into my soft curves.

I came in a soundless scream, too overwhelmed to let air pass through my vocal cords. Pleasure unlike any I had felt before convulsed through me. Kristos leaned forward to kiss me on the neck, my legs pressing into my belly and chest until I could barely breathe. I flinched as I felt the sting of his fangs piercing my skin, but that was quickly replaced by the added pleasure of feeling his cock spasming inside me in rhythm with his feeding.

The way he held me was almost like being hog-tied. My body was wrapped in his, pinned by his weight which also immobilized my legs. All I had were my hands, which sometimes gripped the sheets or ran through the soft hair on his head. If the stitches bothered me, I didn't notice any longer. In the midst of my orgasm, I had held onto the meat of his shoulders, shuddering against him.

When he was done, he seized my mouth in another kiss and I tasted my salt and blood on his lips. With tentative laps of my tongue, I cleaned the traces of our lovemaking from his mouth.

Kristos rolled off me with a sigh of contentment.

Seeking reassurance, I asked, "Did I pass inspection?"

He pulled me close, snuggling me against his shoulder. "Yes, you were fine."

"Fine?" I half sat up to look at him. Fine didn't seem like an enthusiastic endorsement.

He laughed. "You were the best virgin I ever had for dinner."

The absurdity of his response was not reassuring. "That's it, just a good meal?"

He went quiet for a moment. "More than a meal, Myra." He planted a kiss on the top of my head. "There's something about you, who you are, the way you taste that makes me want more." He fell silent again. "Tell me about your parents."

I gave him a confused look. "Why?"

"It might explain why I'm so besotted with you. You don't taste like the other girls."

A coy smile danced on my lips. He'd said besotted and that made me happy. Very happy. I liked the idea of being able to besot a man like Kristos. "My mom, her name is Elena. She's Irish-American with the blue eyes and red hair. My dad, well, all I know is his name. He didn't stick around. His name was Devon Desanto."

Kristos froze, going still as death. "You're sure about that?"

I frowned. "Yes, why? Do you know him?" The idea was preposterous, but something I'd said had caused Kristos to react strongly.

"Seriously, Myra, are you certain that's his name?" His eyes caught mine in a fierce gaze that took my breath away.

Mute, I nodded. Whatever it was, my gut instinct told me it was bad. Kristos had been happy when I'd confessed to being a virgin. That happy face was gone, now replaced by a serious one that carried an edge of worry.

He pushed me away and sat up, his brow furrowed. "We've met." He hit the bed with a fist. "That's who you reminded me of. I can taste him in you."

I stared at my hands, but saw nothing other than very

normal skin. "Are you serious? I taste like my father? Do you have any idea how weird that sounds?" I looked at Kristos then, utterly confused. "And how does that even work? Do vampires go around just randomly fanging people?"

Kristos gave an apologetic shrug. "We rarely share our blood, but I swore a blood oath once, a long time ago during one of our wars. He no longer has any claim on me, but you never forget tasting someone as powerful as he was. Vampires called him The Maker."

I shook my head and moved to sit next to him, pulling the sheet with me to cover my nakedness. "Seriously? You really knew my dad? And he's The Maker? Of what?" The questions tumbled out in a rush, reflecting the chaos in my mind. "Wait. Are you saying my dad was a vampire?"

"Yes. Your father is a vampire. An ancient, powerful one. And I knew him once. Vampires live so long, we all meet one another sooner or later."

My father was a vampire? What? I frowned and rubbed my forehead trying to make sense of everything. Losing my virginity was not supposed to end in a paternity test. This wasn't some cheesy talk show, it was my life, but everything had gone Jerry Springer on me anyways.

What the hell?

How had the father I never met suddenly become relevant How did it turn out he was a vampire? I couldn't believe it.

Kristos crossed his arms, a thoughtful expression on his

face, reflecting he wasn't the only one trying to process the news. "The thing is, knowing he's your father, I don't think I was the target that night at the restaurant."

I blinked at him, unsure of how much more I could take. "What are you saying?"

His eyes locked with mine again. "It was you they wanted."

"Me?" My voice was a squeak now. I clutched the sheet tight in my hands. "Who would want me dead?"

"Your father's enemies," he said his voice flat. "Or perhaps opportunists looking to build up their power base."

I put a hand to my forehead to try and stop the panic swirling inside. "Kristos, please make sense. I don't understand."

"I thought there was something about your blood that seemed familiar, but I couldn't place it." He tapped his chin with a finger, thinking. "The attack...well, I never suspected they would want you. You're human."

"What does my father's name have to do with this? I've never even met the guy. He's missed every milestone in my life and now he's causing people to shoot at me? It's all so random."

"Your father is one of the first vampires that ever walked." Kristos' eyes caught mine again. "The last time I saw him, he was going by Devon Desanto. It can't be a coincidence."

"Oh my God." My words came out in breathless gasps. With one trembling finger I touched my teeth, checking for fangs. Just in case I'd failed to notice them these past twenty-five years. "What are you getting at, Kristos? Why would they want *me*?"

"You're his blood and some would do anything to have you."

"Alive or dead?" I couldn't keep a small quiver out of my voice. The things Kristos said terrified me.

He nodded. "That would depend on their agenda."

I took a deep breath. "So half the vampire world wants to shoot me and the other half wants to kidnap me?" It sounded insane. This couldn't be real.

He gripped my shoulders and gave me a little shake. "You don't understand, you have the blood of the old ones in you. Whoever has you would control you and add to their power."

"Making me the most valuable pawn on the board. Is that it?" I didn't play much chess, but the analogy seemed to fit.

"Yes."

We were both silent for a moment. Kristos watched me, his expression contemplative while I tried not to hyperventilate. This was just too much information. I couldn't take it all in.

"Wait," I said as a thought occurred to me. "If my dad's a vampire does that mean vampires can have babies?"

Kristos shook his head. "No. The Maker was special. Somehow undead yet still able to make life. There's no other vampire like him and that's what makes you so special."

I blinked some more, struggling to absorb it all. "Do I have brothers and sisters?"

He shrugged. "I don't know. It's possible."

"That's just crazy. I don't believe any of it." I crossed my arms, holding on to myself as my heart raced like a cornered animal. "It was just one shooting. How do we even know it has anything to do with me?"

He wrapped an arm around me and I leaned into his strength. "I know vampires, Myra. They've found you through your father and what happened at the restaurant is only the beginning. It's true, no matter how much you want to deny it. The real question is, how do I keep you safe?"

"I'll just go home and act like nothing happened." In fact, I would go right now and dive deep under the covers of my bed where no one could see me.

He shook his head. "That won't stop them. You're not thinking clearly, Myra. They're on to you now and won't give up until you're theirs."

"What do you suggest then?" I pushed him away and moved to the opposite side of the bed.

He made no move to follow, giving me space. "Let me bring you over."

I clutched at my throat, eyes wide. "Make me a vampire?"

He nodded. "It would make you stronger, faster and put you under my protection. That would stop most of this madness."

I frowned. "Most? Not all?"

Kristos shrugged. "Vampires can be very determined, especially the old ones, but I can protect you."

I said nothing for several long minutes and Kristos didn't push me. "Is this really the only way?" I wasn't sure I was ready to die and be reborn with a bloodsucking habit.

Before he could respond, the now familiar sound of bullets thudding into the wall hit our ears. I rolled off the bed, dropping to the floor. Kristos followed me, landing on top of my body.

"This is happening?" My voice came out in a panicked shriek. "Again?"

Thud-thud-thud. More bullets sounded.

Kristos remained calm and dragged me over to the wall where he pushed an unseen button. A panel in the wall swished open and he pushed me through into a dark room. Once I was inside, he entered and hit another unseen button to shut the panel. After fumbling in the dark for a moment, he found the light switch and flipped it on.

A dim light illuminated a small room with metal walls. A bank of video monitors on one wall flared to life showing the apartment was full of armed operatives dressed in all black. Kristos watched them with a frown and went to a control panel by the door we'd come in through and hit some buttons. There was the reassuring sound of bolts sliding home and locks clicking in place. "There, we're the only ones who can open the door now."

Then he turned his attention to a storage bin set next to the door. Quickly rummaging through its contents he pulled out some clothes and tossed them to me.

"Here, put something on."

"Where are we?" I kept my voice to a whisper, not wanting anyone to hear us in our hidey-hole. Sorting through the clothes, I found a t-shirt and pulled it on, grateful for its warmth.

"It's a panic room. We'll be safe here."

Relief made me weak. Wrapping my arms around myself, I watched the monitors. The apartment was overrun and all the black clothing made it look like an invasion of ants...that happened to carry semi-automatic weapons. "What about your people?"

He grimaced. "Dead, hiding or running. I won't know until this is over."

I gulped. "Who are they? What do they want?"

"I don't know who they are, yet, but I'm fairly certain they're here for one thing. You." His expression was grim as he watched the men ransack the room I'd stayed in after the first shooting.

"And the only way to stop this madness is for me to become a vampire?" I couldn't believe I was even asking such a question. It sounded beyond insane when I said it out loud.

"Correct."

"Have you ever brought anyone over?"

He nodded. "Yes."

"Does it hurt?"

Another nod.

Whatever I was about to say died on my lips as something on the monitor caught my eye. The blonde vampire who'd brought me clothes earlier was walking down the hallway toward Kristos' room, pushing a hooded figure in front of her. With the hood over the woman's face, it was hard to be certain, but the gaunt, feminine frame looked familiar.

"Oh, God," I said. I knew there was a good reason I hadn't liked that woman.

"What? What is it?" Kristos reached out to touch me as if searching for a physical wound.

I pointed to the monitor bank. "I think she has my mom."

Kristos swore under his breath and slammed the wall with his hand.

"Isn't she one of yours?" I asked just as she waved forward a bunch of the men. They weren't shooting at her and my heart sank.

"Not anymore, apparently." Kristos' voice was terse.

I narrowed my eyes at him. "What does that mean?"

"I brought her over and she should be mine, but there are ways to take over someone's kin, to become their master. It appears Samira has been stolen from me. Her loyalties lie elsewhere now."

"What do we do now?" I asked unable to keep the panic from my voice. Vampires were supposed to save my mom, but my current circumstances made cancer look safe.

"They're trying to draw you out, make you reveal yourself."

"And if I don't?"

He looked at me, eyes filled with regret. "Your mom will become expendable."

I put a hand over my mouth and tears gathered in my eyes.

"It's my life for hers, isn't it?"

He nodded. "I'm afraid so."

My lower lip trembled and the tears spilled down my cheeks. On the monitor, I could see that mom was in Kristos' bedroom now. The blonde vampire shoved her onto the bed and then stalked around the room, hitting the walls as she went.

"She knows we're in here, doesn't she?" I flinched as the vampire in question put some muscle into her hits. I fully expected her fist to punch through the wall into our safe haven. Fortunately, the walls held.

His lips thinned and he glared at the video monitor. "She was part of my team. She would know about the panic room."

"Is there any good news?"

Kristos shook his head. "Not much. We're safe in here, but your mom is out there. I assume you're not interested in sacrificing her?"

"God, no!"

We both fell silent watching the blond vampire try to tear down the walls of Kristos' bedroom. She ripped out the drywall and cast it aside like she was peeling an egg as she tried to reach us.

"I have an idea," Kristos said. "It's risky, but I think we can make it work." He leaned in for a kiss saying only, "Drink."

I started to ask him 'drink what?' but blood poured into my open mouth. He'd cut his tongue with his fangs, I realized. I tried to push him away, but his hands gripped my shoulders like steel.

"Drink of me, love."

"Are you going to turn me now?"

He lifted his head. "No, I would never force that on you, but I'm going to make it look like I did and buy us some time. They'll back off if they think I've made you my kin. Now drink as much as you can."

His lips tried to claim mine again but I turned my head. "But they took Samira, right? What's to stop them from taking me anyway?"

He wiped blood off his mouth. "Samira was always weak. I should have never made her. Right now they think you're weak, too. They think they can take you because you haven't been turned yet, that none of our kind have any hold over you. The second I prove that assumption wrong, the game changes."

A wry smile played across his lips. "Not to mention the idea of you as a vampire, one they aren't master of, will give them pause. Your father was one of the most powerful of our kind. There is no doubt you will be powerful, too. It's your birthright. As a human, you are theirs for the taking. You'll never be able to run fast enough or fight back. But if you're a vampire..."

"I *can* run fast enough and fight back," I finished for him.

He nodded. "And you'll have all of my resources and power at your disposal. I won't let them take you."

"Why? Why do you care? Why are you doing this for me?" He'd been a gentleman since we'd first met, but even chivalry had limits. He'd saved me, protected me and cared when we barely knew each other. "You don't owe me anything."

"It's not about what I owe you. I didn't lose my sense of right and wrong when I became a vampire." He grimaced. "Some vampires lose themselves to their immortality. They think, if you live forever nothing really matters."

"Does it?"

"I believe it matters even more. We become the choices we make. I try not to forget that."

"So you're a saint as well as vampire."

Another wry smile played across his lips. "I doubt the church would agree with you on that. Now, we are running out of time. Are you ready?"

I nodded. As his lips covered mine yet again, I hoped everything he'd told me was true. That my life hung on every word he'd uttered terrified me, but I gave his plan everything I had, doing my best to swallow his salty blood. It hit my stomach like lead and a wave of nausea almost over took me. I made a gagging sound as my throat recoiled.

Kristos' grip on my shoulders tightened in warning. "This is our only chance to save your mom. You have to keep it down."

After what seemed hours of suckling his tongue, he broke contact. Sweeping my hair to one side, he exposed my throat. "Now a fresh bite at your neck to make it look authentic." I bit my lip hard enough to draw blood as his fangs pierced my skin. This was no intimate foreplay like all the other feedings. There was no arousal to blunt the pain and I whimpered as he sucked at my neck.

Fortunately, he didn't feed long and a moment later he let me go. I reeled at the absence of his arms to steady me and my stomach heaved, threatening to reject his blood. I huddled against the wall, gasping for air.

"Look at me." He helped me stand and lifted my chin to meet his eyes. "I'm going to put you into a light sleep. Just look into my eyes."

I wanted to ask him about clichéd vampire powers, but there was no time. The blonde vampire had found the button opening the door to the panic room. It didn't work, of course, but I could hear the click of the door trying to open and then jamming up against the internal locks Kristos had triggered.

One second, I was looking into his eyes thinking how beautiful they were, the next I knew nothing as they cast me into a dark oblivion.

8

I woke some time later. I was in Kristos' bed and when I turned to my side, I found my mother next to me. The hood had been removed and she was asleep, breathing deeply as she dreamed.

Sitting up, I stretched my arms over head, wincing at a throbbing pain in my wrist. Looking at it, I saw two neat puncture marks. I'd been bitten, but why or by who I didn't know.

Frowning I scanned the room for Kristos, but he wasn't there. I cocked my head to the side and listened, hearing only silence. No gun shots, which was reassuring.

Wanting to be cautious, I ducked back into the panic room, which was still open, and checked the video monitors. The armed men were gone, but the apartment was a mess of overturned furniture and there were bullet holes everywhere.

Movement on one of the screens caught my eye and I watched as Kristos appeared along with the blonde vampire. I leaned forward and by chance hit a button that turned on the sound, allowing me to overhear their conversation.

Kristos held the blonde's arms pinned behind her back. "The only reason I let you live, Samira, is to carry the truth back to your new master. She's mine. I've claimed her. You've tasted it."

Samira gave him a defiant look over her shoulder. "I will tell him all that I saw and of the blood that I drank, but the truth will only be proven when she rises."

Looking at my wrist, I wondered if that was the blood she was referring to me. What was going on?

"She will rise," said Kristos, his voice ringing with authority.

Samira shrugged, her expression insolent. "Your eternity will be forfeit if she doesn't."

"Don't threaten me." He wrapped a hand around her throat. "I made you, I can unmake you."

"You made me weak and ripe for the taking. Watch that my new master doesn't take her too," she said with a snarl.

In response, he spun her around to face him. Lifting her by the throat until her feet dangled in the air he walked into the main living area of the apartment. I tracked his movements from the camera in the hallway to the one that showed the living room. With a harsh yell, he threw Samira against the glass window. The glass shuddered but held.

He picked Samira up for round two, whipping her into the air by her hair and back against the glass. It cracked this time with an audible snapping sound. Another hit and it shattered and Samira flew out the window, arms and legs flailing.

Kristos stood at the edge of the broken window and watched her fall, a look of grim determination on his face. A group of men rushed into the apartment and my stomach clenched with fear. They fanned out through the apartment and I searched the console for some kind of alert button but couldn't find one. I was just about to go drag my mom into the panic room and lock the door behind us when the men hailed Kristos.

"Are you okay, boss?" one of them asked.

"We came as soon as we got the alert," said another.

The men all had their weapons drawn and scanned the room for threats.

Kristos rubbed the back of his neck. "The threat has been neutralized for now." He gestured out the window. "Someone took Samira from me. She's on her way to report to her new master. Have her followed, but be careful."

"Yes, sir," said the tallest of the group. His height seemed to correlate to some authority as he quickly gestured to two men who gave a curt nod before jumping out the window after Samira. I guess vampires don't mind jumping off buildings.

My mother gave a groan and I rushed to her side just as Kristos walked into the bedroom. My mom's eyes fluttered open and she sat up. "Where am I ?" She caught sight of me. "Myra."

"Mom." I sat on the edge of the bed and gave her a hug. "Are you okay?"

"Yes." Her brow furrowed. "I was kidnapped."

I rubbed her back. "I know. I think we're okay now though." I turned to Kristos. "It's over, right?"

He gave a slow nod. "For the moment."

I sighed in relief. "Thank God."

Kristos offered me his hand and, when I took it, he pulled me into a hug. Putting his mouth to my ear, he whispered. "You're not safe yet, love. You may never be safe, not while you're human. I'm afraid if you want to live, you will have to die."

I sank into his embrace as the truth of his words washed over me. Every choice I had involved death. I could die and lose my mom. I could turn into a vampire and protect her...maybe. Plus she still had cancer and wasn't in the clear yet. Nothing was certain except someone would die. The idea terrified me.

"Will you help me, Kristos?" I asked in a soft voice.

"You drank of me and we are blood bound now. I will do everything I can." He planted a chaste kiss on my cheek. "The apartment is not secure. We need to leave."

So we gathered up my mom. I threw some clothes into a bag, and we ran into the night. Kristos had said he wouldn't turn me against my will, but my life wasn't leaving me much choice. I wasn't free or safe. I wondered if I ever would be again.

The best I could hope for was some time to make peace with the future being forced upon me and come to terms with a past I had never known.

9

SEVERAL DAYS LATER...

If you want to live, you will have to die.

Turning Kristos' words over and over in my mind, I sipped my caramel latte amidst the hustle and bustle of a very busy coffee shop in New York's Upper East Side. Fall had decided to give everyone a surprise preview of winter and the crisp air drove people into the small cafe. I watched as they ordered their favorite brew in harsh New York accents and waited for their orders, hands thrust in pockets because the weather had shifted so suddenly that no one had gloves yet.

Yesterday it had been seventy, but today the temperature had dropped to the thirties. They left the shop in self-important whirls of too light coats and hands wrapped around steaming takeout cups, soaking up the heat. What I wouldn't give for such an easy solution to the chill permeating my life.

In the days since I'd been attacked for a second time and my mother had been kidnapped nothing much had been resolved. For the moment we were safe. Kristos and I were holed up in a faded but respectable apartment while my mom was in a clinic receiving state-of-the-art medical care. Unfortunately, there was no future in mere safety. We hadn't solved my problems, only hit the pause button on them. I couldn't go back to school or move forward with my life until we reached a better resolution than simply being good at hiding.

I sighed and looked up at the cafe menu, debating whether to have an espresso too. Vampires kept me up late these days and my caffeine consumption had increased accordingly. That's when I noticed a dark, swarthy man standing in line watching me intently. He had handsome Italian looks with chocolate gelato eyes and sleek black hair.

When he kept looking at me, I slouched down in my chair, pulling the collar of my coat up to hide my face. It was better if no one noticed me too much. Way too many people would like to know where I was and whether or not I was dead already, and if I was still alive, they would be only too happy to rectify that oversight.

Undeterred by the shield of my coat, the stranger continued to stare at me as if he recognized me from somewhere and then abruptly answered his phone, turning his back to me as he spoke. Shaking his head as if irritated, he rushed out of the cafe without even placing an order. I held my breath as he went and didn't let it out until the door shut after him. He hadn't bothered to look at me again so it must've just been a coincidence. Maybe I looked like an old girlfriend. That could happen, right? Surely not *everyone* was out to get me? But I couldn't shake a little niggle of suspicion. His expression had been sharply intent.

My hands shook slightly as I finished my latte. I probably shouldn't have even come to the coffee shop, but I was going stir-crazy sitting in the apartment. I needed a change of scenery.

Every afternoon for the last few days, I'd been sneaking down here for a quick caffeine fix. Kristos' security relaxed when the sun was at its zenith and I could slip out without raising any alarms. It helped that there was an ATM directly across the street from the apartment building, which made it easy to get cash.

I never had enough cash, which was why I'd signed up to be a blood courtesan in the first place—out of financial desperation. Selling sex mixed with blood to vampires was supposed to have been a fast way to earn a large amount of cash for mom's medical care. Not to mention it had been the only way to raise funds I could find outside of a bank heist. I didn't have the skill-set to rob banks, but I did have blood. It only seemed logical to trade on what assets I had in order to help my mom.

In hindsight, I probably should've robbed a bank.

I shook my head and gazed deep into my now empty coffee cup. How was I supposed to have known how dangerous vampires could be? Or that I was the top prize in some bizarre game of the 'sins of the father are visited upon his children?' The only reason I'd survived so far was because of Kristos.

Just the thought of the handsome vampire sent a tingle through me. In the back of my mind the connection that we shared ever since I'd drank his blood flared to life. I could feel him as if he was right there and pressed up against me. He was sleeping at the moment. While he could walk during the day, he preferred to sleep until the sun set.

Part of the reason why security was so lax during daylight hours was because he was the exception to the rule. The last week and a half had been a crash course in vampires. I'd learned most vampires didn't have a choice about when they were up and about. The sun came up and they powered down like someone had abruptly removed their batteries. I'd seen it happen to the men Kristos had brought in to protect me. One second they were awake, and the next they were the equivalent of a poseable doll.

As far as he knew, Kristos was the only day walker of his kind. "We are just like humans, Myra," he'd said with a sardonic smile, his blue eyes glittering with a mixture of amusement and restrained impatience at my constant stream of questions. "We're all different."

"Can some of you fly?" I'd asked, idly running my hand over his chest. We'd been in bed—we were *always* in bed—and I loved to touch him. He was smooth and hard, like a river rock molded by forces of nature I couldn't comprehend.

He'd shrugged and ran his hand down my back, reciprocating. "I've heard rumors but never seen it myself."

I'd traced the outline of his pecs, biting my lip as his nipples hardened at the attention. I loved his chest. "Turn into bats?"

Kristos had shaken his head. "No shape shifting that I'm aware of."

I smiled at the memory of that conversation. I'd peppered him with so many questions, he'd finally silenced me with a long, drawn out kiss that completely changed the subject.

He was a good kisser and an amazing lover, so I'd allowed him to distract me. But during the day, when he wasn't there to divide my focus, all the unanswered questions swarmed my mind, stinging me with anxiety and worry.

I gripped my coffee cup a little tighter, wincing when it pulled at the stitches in my hand, an unwanted souvenir from the first time someone tried to kill me. I tilted my coffee cup up toward the ceiling as I drank, wanting the last few drops that had collected at the bottom. As I waited for it to flow to my mouth, I scanned the cafe once more, peering out over the cup's brim. There were maybe five people in the coffee shop now, noses buried in their laptops or smart phones. No one cared about me.

I relaxed marginally then, and contemplated the pastries in the display case. A brownie the size of my hand beckoned me with its glistening chocolate ganache icing. My stomach growled at the sight of it.

Sad, but true: When I died, my ability to eat brownies would die with me. That fact had been established fairly early on in my questioning.

My priorities quickly rearranged themselves to include a brownie, a cinnamon scone and a gingersnap that was bigger than the brownie. If I ate it all in one sitting I invited diabetes and a five pound weight gain, but those kinds of health consequences weren't much of a concern anymore.

Some people might call that an upside to my situation, but I was too wound up about things to take it as a plus. It was more stress eating than anything else.

I took the sugary confections to go, and clutching the bag against my chest, I made my way back to the apartment. As I went, I scanned both in front of me and behind me for sinister figures or signs of being followed. I hadn't seen any cause for concern on my previous jaunts to the coffee shop and today was no different. If I was on the vampire world's most wanted list, they weren't working too hard to find me.

The safe house wasn't as nice as the penthouse suite Kristos had taken me to after the first shooting. I shook my head recalling how we'd both thought they were after him, neither of us realizing it was me they wanted until it was almost too late. My absentee father had made me a hot commodity among the fanged set.

The apartment building was in the same block as the coffee shop, but on the opposite end. So it only took a few minutes to walk back. Just as I was about to step into the entrance, a cadre of armed men dressed in black spilled down the sidewalk on the other side of the street. They tried to look casual, but the way they scanned the street—as if they were looking for something and knew exactly how to find it—made me nervous. They walked with a purpose and every so often their hands would go to their sides as if reaching for a gun.

I ducked inside the building and pulled the door shut after me. Thankfully, the glass foyer of the building was tinted—you could see out, but not in. Another plus, access required a key card. Unless they were willing to shoot out the glass, they wouldn't get in. I worried my bottom lip and watched them gather round the ATM I had used to withdraw cash a few days ago.

One of the men seemed to sense my presence and turned his head sharply, zeroing in on my building. He was blonde with an ugly red scar down the side of his face. His gaze seemed to penetrate the tinted glass.

With a gasp I stepped back. My heart raced as adrenaline shot through me, ready for fight-or-flight. My hand shaking, I pressed the key card against the access pad for the second door and rushed inside to the main lobby. When I looked back, the man was still there, watching, but one of his buddies nudged him forward. With a frown, he moved along with the rest of his group.

They spread out as they went, with a few crossing to my side of the street. I could see now that they had earpieces and were communicating with each other. I fled before they reached my door, eschewing the elevator for the stairs. Climbing all twenty flights was out of the question, but I didn't want to be found waiting for an elevator on the main floor if they somehow gained entry.

By the tenth flight of stairs, my heart pounded like it would explode and my breathing was loud and labored. I staggered into the hallway, thighs burning, and headed for the elevator. It was Kristos who made me think of things like taking the stairs. He helped me keep up with my new action-adventure life style.

"Be ready at all times," he'd said to me time and time again. "Zig when they think you'll zag," was another favorite line.

Hopefully I'd zagged while they were looking for a zig. I shivered even as the sweat trickled down my back from my impromptu workout. That had been close. *I should probably stay in for the next few days.*

10

The elevator delivered me to the top floor with a soft ding. The doors opened and I jumped because Kristos was standing there, waiting for me.

"Hey, Kristos." I stepped into the hallway and tried to sound nonchalant.

"Myra," he said, his voice almost a growl. He took my elbow, fingers digging into me with disapproval, and guided me back to the apartment.

"What are you doing up so early?" I asked, feigning innocence. He was not going to be happy about me sneaking out or the black ops team infiltrating the area. I wanted to delay the bad news as long as I could.

He shoved me through the entrance to our living quarters—a four bedroom with a rather mundane view of the street below. We slept in one bedroom and the rest of his team shared the other three. For a wealthy CEO like Kristos, I imagined it was like living in a trailer park.

"You woke me up," he said.

"I did?" I thought back to all the times his name had come to mind, wondering which of them had drawn him to consciousness. I still wasn't used to the link between us. In fact, I hadn't even noticed it at first. Now, I could feel it, but didn't know how it worked. Baby steps, I guess.

"The bond we share," he gestured to himself and then me, "means I can track you, know what you are feeling."

"Oh." I paused wondering how that felt during sex. Did he feel the desire rising in me? Could I feel his? I would have to try it the next time we made love.

"I saw the men on the street from the window. They're looking for you, tracing your debit card. You know you weren't supposed to leave the apartment and now they know you're here." His tone was full of reproof.

I opened my mouth to defend my disobedience, but nothing came out. Kristos was right to be upset. Finally, I asked, "How did you know about the debit card?"

"Because they wouldn't have looked twice at the ATM otherwise. You used it to withdraw cash for your little outing, correct?" At my nod, he gave a long suffering sigh. Grabbing my purse, he pulled out my wallet and flipped through it until he located my bank card. Holding it up so I could see, he crushed it in his hand. He didn't even grimace either. Vampires were stronger than humans, I knew that, but it always chilled me to see it up close and personal. He'd thrown Samira out a skyscraper window like she weighed nothing and then the vampire had gotten up and walked off like nothing had happened. She'd only been allowed to live so she could tell her new master that I was a vampire. We were counting on that lie to keep me safe. If everyone believed I'd already been claimed, it made me less of a target. In theory at least.

He opened his hand to reveal my now crumpled debit card. "It's just luck that you weren't found. As it is, we're going to have to move tonight. We can't stay here now that they've traced us to this area. You took a big risk, Myra." Kristos took the bag of pastries from me and opened it. He wrinkled his nose at the sugary scent that rose in the air. "Is this worth it?"

I thought of the chocolate brownie with its luscious ganache icing and gave a half shrug. In an attempt at levity, I said, "Asks the man who was born before chocolate was invented."

"No, asks the man who is trying to save your life. At great personal cost, I might add." He was irritated now and fisted his hands in my hair, pulling me in for a stern, admonishing kiss. While he kissed me, he took my purse and dropped it to the floor. The bakery bag followed suit and he paused just long enough to give me *a look*.

"What? I was hungry." I did my best to look innocent and my stomach growled on cue.

He bared his fangs at me, but smiled as he did so. "You left *me* with nothing to eat."

"I came back, didn't I?"

"You were never supposed to go out in the first place." His

eyes narrowed. "You realize both our lives are at stake?"

I evaded his gaze. One, he could play mind tricks on me if I looked at him too long, and two, I didn't want him to see that I felt guilty. "I was going crazy in the apartment."

"Go crazy or go dead, your choice, love. Just try not to take me with you." He kissed me again and pulled my coat off my shoulders, using it to pin my arms behind my back. "You smell delicious, by the way. What did you eat?"

"Just a caramel latte." I lifted my head to look up at him, aware that the small movement exposed my throat.

He sniffed the nape of my neck, burying his nose there, his fangs just pricking my skin. "The contrast between bitter and sweet is tantalizing."

"Mmm," I moaned as I pressed up against his fangs, wanting them to break my skin. I welcomed the pain; it meant I was still alive. Also, the things he did to me while feeding were pretty spectacular.

He refused to bite and pulled back, releasing me as he did so. "I could have sent someone out for your latte."

I shook my head and removed my coat, draping it over a dining room chair. The compact apartment layout had the dining room just inside the entrance. "It's not the same." I'd wanted the freedom to pretend everything was normal. 'Pretend' being the key word. I was probably in the denial phase of my life going to hell.

"A bullet to the head isn't any fun either." He made a gun with his finger and aimed it at me. "They'll either shoot you, bury you or make you rise to their bidding like a slave. Is that what you want?"

I sighed. "It's just the suspense is killing me. Sitting here feels like a mistake."

His expression became serious. "I can turn you tonight."

I gulped, the offer making my blood run cold. To his credit, Kristos was giving me a lot of space and time to try and process the inevitable. He'd also set my mom up with medical care in a first class clinic under an assumed name to protect her. He was an all around gentleman...if that could be said for a bloodsucking vampire. I trusted him, except for when I didn't.

I also wasn't so sure about this 'become a vampire' thing.

He gave me a fatherly kiss on the forehead. "You're going to have to decide soon, Myra. I can't keep you safe forever."

I leaned against him. "Thank you for trying though."

He hugged me and then his hands began to roam my curves. His fingers tugged at the buttons on my blouse.

I put up a hand to stop him. "What are you doing?"

"I'm up. I'm hungry. We have no place to go and some free time before the others wake. In short, we are alone and I plan to take full advantage of that fact." A wicked grin spread across his mouth as he spoke. "Consider this your punishment for breaking the rules."

I arched an eyebrow. "You're letting me off lightly."

"That," he peeled my shirt away from my chest, exposing my bra, "remains to be seen."

Kristos led me to the bedroom we shared, discarding my clothes as we went. By the time we crossed the threshold, I'd lost my shirt, my bra and my pants. He pushed me down on the bed and inched my panties off, tossing them over his shoulder.

I reached for him, wanting to undo his shirt, but he evaded my touch. "Not yet, love. Look into my eyes."

I hesitated. "That's such a cliché. I can't believe you just said that."

He chuckled. "Just look into my eyes, Myra."

"What if I don't want to?"

Kristos ran his hands along my stomach and up to cup my breasts. I shivered as he caressed their sensitive tips. "You'll be missing out."

I made the mistake of looking up and making eye contact, wanting to see his face. His gaze captured mine in less than a second. I now knew that he'd been doing this to me since we met. I'd naively thought his eyes were irresistible because they were sparkling aquamarine blue, but it really was whatever magic that made a vampire a vampire. I'd been a virgin on a few different levels when I first met Kristos.

"Come for me, Myra." His voice sounded distant and distorted as if he spoke underwater. My body however, heard him crystal clear and bucked as a hard, fast orgasm washed over me. The whole time our eyes were locked on each other, the windows to our souls wide open. His were full of darkness that threatened to spill out and consume me. I imagined mine were like those of a doe cornered by a hunter, wide and brimming with shattered innocence.

Kristos allowed me a second to recover and once my breathing had resumed at its normal rate, he said, "You will come every time I command it, understood?"

I gave a slow nod, bowing to his compulsion. A shiver went through me at his forcefulness, the way he just took my body and made it his. Kristos was a considerate man and attentive to my needs...except when it came to sex, then he just took what he wanted, what he needed, without asking. He'd indoctrinated me into a world where blood and sex were one and the same. Now I could never go back.

He broke eye contact then and kissed his way up my body. Swirling his tongue in my belly button, he gave the command. "Come."

My back bowed this time and little shrieking sounds escaped from my throat. He moved up, nuzzling the hollow under my sternum, where my ribcage diverged to separate sides of my body. Making his way to my breast, he paused, mouth poised to take in the nipple, which jutted up in a little salute at the mere promise of his touch.

"Come and come and come," he said just before his mouth closed over my nipple. My body instantly obeyed and pleasure wracked me until I barely felt his fangs pierce my breast. He sucked me as if he were a nursing babe; strong long pulls of his mouth that tugged on my nipple, forcing the blood into his mouth and tightening the wet darkness at my core.

Reading my body like Braille, his hand drifted to the cleft between my legs. Eager, I spread wide for him and his fingers teased the sensitive bud there. Despite the multiple on-command orgasms, I still wanted more. My appetite for him ravaged me like wildfire.

Switching breasts, he did the same on the other side. The orgasms shuddered through me, wringing the moisture out of my body. Sweat broke out on my upper lip and my skin became hot and damp. A seeping wetness pooled at my center and his fingers dipped in and out of it, stoking the heat to a fever pitch. With his hand where it was, my pleasure stretched out for impossibly long plateaus.

He watched my face as he fed. My focus was in and out, like flickering lights in a thunderstorm, but I saw the way his mouth kneaded my breast and how his throat moved as he swallowed my blood.

After he'd fed from both breasts, he left the bed to remove his clothes, revealing a sculpted physique that would have made Michelangelo swoon. Then he parted my legs and his hard length pressed against my wet entrance. My hips thrust up, wanting all of him already.

That made him smile and go all the slower, teasing me. I whimpered and reached for him, trying to pull him in, but he danced away from my grasp. He claimed me inch by tortuous inch, a pace that left my core desperate to be filled. When he finally sank all the way inside me, I groaned with satisfaction.

"How many times do you want to come?" he asked.

"It's up to you." With a finger, I caught a drop of blood from my breast and pressed it against his lips, giving myself to him completely. He sucked my finger into his mouth, fangs scraping over my knuckle.

Releasing my finger, he said, "Come."

I arched, gasping as the wave rushed me, pebbling my nipples as it went. Before I'd returned to earth, while I was still swept away, he had me come again. Then again.

It seemed as if my body's capacity for pleasure was endless. There was no sense of fatigue or any fading of my response. I came for him every time like it was the first orgasm. The heaviness in my limbs, though, and the way they shook when I tried to move belied my fatigue, but I didn't really feel it. I was too caught up in Kristos' eyes, his touch and the way he filled me to the point of bursting.

Kristos leaned down and bit my neck when he reached his own climax. Before his fangs slid through my skin as if I was made of water, he paused to whisper, "Come for me, Myra."

I screamed, my hands digging into his shoulders. The orgasm bucked through me fierce as a wild horse, threatening to trample me into oblivion.

When he finished, he rolled to my side. I remained frozen in place, trembling as aftershocks zapped my system. My mind fought to maintain awareness. All I wanted to do was sink into the soft darkness of sleep, but one simple sound put me on hyper alert.

Someone was knocking on the door. Not our bedroom door, which would not have alarmed me at all as it would have been one of Kristos' men. No, the knocking came from the front door.

Not only did no one know where we were, they shouldn't be in the building let alone on our floor without being buzzed in. An adrenaline surge burned away all my lethargy and I bolted out of bed, every muscle taut, my ears straining.

Kristos responded in kind and we both stood in tense silence willing the knock to have been a fluke. It wasn't. The knock came again, more insistent this time. Whoever was out there knew the apartment was occupied.

This was bullets-are-probably-about-to-fly bad.

Kristos frowned. "Get dressed and stay here until I give the all clear." He pulled on his pants and snagged his gun from the bedside table.

I didn't know anything about guns other than his was sleek and black and that I wished I had one. For once, I'd like to be the one doing the shooting. I hated feeling so defenseless.

Kristos left, shutting our bedroom door after him. I got dressed and then cracked the door open which gave me a clear view of the apartment's entrance. Kristos was peering through the peephole.

I heard a muffled voice speaking from the other side of the door. I was too far away to make out what was said, but Kristos seemed to understand it just fine. Holding the gun behind him and out of sight, he opened the front door.

A tall man with swarthy dark features stepped into the apartment. I gasped, covering my mouth with my hand. It was the man from the coffee shop. Shit. I'd been spotted.

The man's eyes, black as night, scanned the apartment and found me within seconds. He gave a feral smile and beckoned me forward. "Ah, there you are, my tesoro. Come out where we can talk, eh?"

His voice carried in the apartment, a baritone with an accent so thick it almost sounded like he was choking on English. I looked to Kristos for guidance and he nodded, his expression one of resignation. Whoever this man was, he was no stranger and no immediate threat given that Kristos hadn't shot him on sight. I stepped out into the living room, careful to keep my gaze averted. I wasn't sure yet if this stranger could do to me what Kristos did with his eyes and I didn't want to find out either.

"You're up early, Arlo," Kristos said, his voice carefully neutral.

Arlo waved a languid hand. "I can meet the sun when the situation requires." He gave me an arch look which I saw in my peripheral vision. "Even go out for coffee and play the human."

I frowned, angry at myself. I'd been such an idiot to think coffee was worth this risk. It wasn't.

"How did you find us?" Kristos crossed the room to stand next to me. Instinctively I edged closer to him, almost bumping him with my shoulder. He gave me a warning look and stepped to the side. With a start, I realized I'd been blocking his gun hand.

Arlo shrugged. "The council has spies everywhere, but I have more spies than the council."

I raised an eyebrow. "Council?"

"Ah yes, tesoro. Has Kristos not told you? The council is our governing body. They are quite interested in your progeny here. As am I." His studied me while I stared fixedly at the carpet. "She's lovely. Looks like her father."

"You know my father?" I couldn't keep the eagerness from my voice. I'd wondered about him all my life, even more so now that who he was had resulted in a blood price on my head.

"He is my maker, tesoro." Arlo gave a little bow. "We are blood you and I. Brother and sister, albeit in an untraditional way."

"What are you doing here?" Kristos growled more than spoke.

"The council is interested to know if your progeny will take after her father. However, I see she has not been turned yet." I risked a quick glance at Arlo and found him looking at me, speculation shining in his eyes. His gaze was heavy and full of power. I quickly focused back on the carpet. I would have to be careful not to be sucked in against my will.

"We're working on it." Kristos' tone was terse.

"You should know some in the council would prefer her as a human. They want to try and breed her."

My mouth dropped open at that and a sense of horror made

my stomach fall. "What?" I couldn't keep from a shrieking a bit.

Arlo sighed as if finding my alarm tiresome. "You are half vampire yet still mortal. It may be that you can birth others like you. You are a tesoro, a treasure."

"Why would they want more like me?" Kristos and I exchanged glances. Mine reflected my surprise, his was full of guarded suspicion.

"To make a better vampire, what else?" Arlo smirked. "But the council does not know all your father's secrets, tesoro. Or else they would not make such a plan."

I crossed my arms to hide the fact that my hands were shaking. Our conversation had delved into the realm of crazy conspiracy theories...about me. The whole thing freaked me out. "Tell me about my father." I forgot myself and looked up at him again, but he wasn't looking at my face.

His eyes were transfixed on my neck. From the heat burning my cheeks, I knew that my heightened emotions had blossomed in a blush from my chest up to my face. It was one of the things that Kristos found most attractive about me. Apparently, Arlo felt the same way.

"You're quite beautiful," he murmured. He raised his hand, extending a finger as if to touch me. I was well out of reach, but cringed anyway.

"Tell me," I said, repeating my question. "Tell me why you're here. Tell me about my father." What I really meant was 'make this go away.'

Arlo strode over to one of the leather armchairs in the small living room. "Very well." Sitting down, he assumed an upright, almost prim posture. He gestured to the chair across from him inviting us to join him, but neither Kristos nor I moved. "I was the first vampire your father made. I was there when his first child was born."

"I have a brother or a sister?" I put a hand over my mouth in shock.

Arlo shook his head. "No, tesoro. I killed it. It was unfit for life." He moved his hands as if twisting a neck. "I killed the others too."

I stared at his hands, a chill running up my spine. For some reason the stitches in my palm began to itch like crazy, as if responding to his words. I curled my fingers into a fist and dug my nails into the wound, fighting the urge to scratch at it frantically.

"Your father has the reputation of bringing forth life, but what is born is twisted beyond hope of survival. Your father charged me with doing what must be done." He clasped his hands in his lap and looked down at them. "For centuries I cleaned up after your father. He always thought the next baby would be different, but they weren't." He raised his head, his dark gaze falling on me. "Not until you."

Feeling the need to sit down then, I sank into a chair across from Arlo.

"It's evolution," said Kristos, more to himself than anyone else. He moved to stand next to me.

Arlo raised a shoulder in a half shrug. "Of a kind perhaps. Vampires have always displayed a diverse range of abilities, just like humans."

Kristos looked at me with wonder. "Myra, you could be something new. The first of a new species. Neither human nor vampire, yet both at the same time."

I held myself tighter and hid my face from both of them. I didn't know who or what I was anymore and that scared me. "Where is my father?"

The dark man gave a sad shrug. "I don't know. I think he might have met the last death. No one's seen him since before you were born."

I whirled around to look at Kristos. "Do you know where my father is?"

He shook his head. "No, sorry, love."

Bowing my head, I asked, "Why are you here then, Arlo? To kill me?" I peeked at him wanting to see his response.

The dark man shook his head. "You are not twisted and malformed like the others, with stumps for limbs. There is no need to kill you, but every need to protect you. I think Kristos will agree with that. I am only sorry I did not know about you before or I would have been there for you."

"What do we do now?" I asked Kristos.

He sighed. "You have to decide what you want. If you turn, you lose all your human potential."

I raised my eyebrows, confused. "I thought the deal was I

had to become a vampire."

He ran a hand through his hair. "I thought so too, but now, maybe not. There's never been someone like you, I'm not sure what the right move is." He was trying not to show emotion, but I caught a glimpse of happiness as he spoke. For some reason, Kristos liked the idea of me being human. Probably so he could keep feeding from me.

"Arlo?" I barely knew the man, didn't know if I trusted him, but I wanted to hear what he had to say. He was the only connection to my father I had. Plus he wasn't fucking or sucking me and was less likely to have a bias. At least I hoped so.

He waved a hand. "You are invaluable either way. It is up to you, tesoro."

"One thing I do know is we can't stay here anymore. We're going to have to move," Kristos gestured to Arlo. "He found us no problem and you brought an entire brigade down the street with your debit card."

"Where will we go?"

He shook his head. "I'm not telling. You have a knack for exposing our location."

I scowled at him, but he didn't budge. Then the doors to the other bedrooms in the apartment opened all at the same time. Vampires were nothing if not punctual about rising the second the sun set.

They quickly observed that things were not normal and filed into the living room on high alert. Two flanked us on either side while one stood guard at the door and the remaining three fanned out behind us.

Kristos turned to give the two men directly behind him quiet directions and they bowed their heads in unison before going into our bedroom. Probably packing us up in anticipation of the next move.

"I'll go with you," Arlo said.

Kristos shook his head. "No. There's too many of us as it is."

"But I can help you."

"How do we know we can trust you?" I asked, crossing my arms.

If I wanted you for myself, you'd be mine already. I'm here because your father would want it. It's nothing more than simple loyalty to my maker." Arlo waved at Kristos. "And I've always been a man of my word. He can vouch for me."

Kristos looked unimpressed. "If you want to help then lay some fake trails around the city. Keep the council busy chasing its tail. Don't let them find her."

Arlo pursed his lips, hands gripping his gloves tightly. He relaxed after a moment and said, "Very well, but I ask one favor in return."

"What?"

"Proof. A taste of her blood."

Kristos' face contorted with anger, but his voice remained tight with control. "No."

Arlo turned his hands palm up in a placating gesture. "I want to be sure she's Devon's. You have to understand as long as I've lived, there has never been a child like Myra."

"You think I'm lying?" I asked, outraged. I was so angry I forgot not to look at him and lifted my head, eyes narrowed in an angry glare. "His name was on my birth certificate."

Arlo nodded. "I'm not saying you're lying, I'm saying I am afraid to believe in you. I thought you were impossible." He held out a hand. "Just one drop and we'll know for sure. You'll have all my resources behind you, helping to keep you safe. And that is no light promise. When Devon disappeared, I became the master of his kin. I am stronger than even the Council. I can protect you...if you will allow it."

I looked at Kristos who shook his head. He didn't want me to do it. I wasn't sure I wanted to do it, but I also wanted to know. There was an outside chance the man on my birth certificate just happened to share the wrong name. The odds were slim, but it could happen. The thought had occurred to me before and left me wondering if I was who everyone thought I was.

Maybe this was all a huge misunderstanding.

"Just one drop?" I wanted to be clear on the terms.

Kristos looked at me, alarmed. "Myra, you can't—"

"One drop," Arlo interrupted. He held up one finger for emphasis.

I moved to step forward and Kristos put a hand on my arm. "I've tasted you both. You are his daughter. There is no question."

Arlo sniffed. "Forgive me if I distrust your memory, Kristos. He was my maker, I know his blood better than you ever will."

I gave Kristos a hard look. "Are you sure it's him? When was the last time you saw him?"

Kristos hesitated and that was all I needed to make up my mind. I shrugged off his hand. "I have to know for sure. Arlo isn't the only one with doubts."

I crossed the room and held out my hand for Arlo, ready for my vampire paternity test. Kristos didn't try to stop me again, but his displeasure showed in the way his fists clenched at his sides.

Arlo's dark eyes gleamed like polished obsidian and I averted my gaze so he couldn't influence me. He gently took my hand in his, tugging me forward slightly. He paused for a moment to gently run a finger over my stitches. "I would have never let this happen, tesoro."

I made a fist to hide the wound and pulled away. Offering him my other hand, I said, "Just get on with it." The man gave me the willies. There was something too slick about him, like I would slip and fall at any second.

Arlo nodded. Baring his fangs, he touched them to my skin of my palm, and then, with a quick movement of his mouth, punched them through. Even though I saw it coming, I winced at the puncture. Being bitten outside of sex was unpleasant. No wonder vampires sexed everyone up, they had to or no one would agree to feed them.

Arlo was true to his word and didn't take much blood, however, I didn't see what he did next coming. Before I could even move to cover the wound in my arm, he stood and swept me into his arms. He pressed gummy lips against mine and forced his tongue into my mouth. The metallic tang of blood assailed my taste buds. Blood filled my mouth, too much to be the remnants of what he'd taken from me. He'd bitten himself and was now forcing his blood on me.

I tried to pull back, but he was vampire strong. It was like trying to move a mountain. Kristos came in and shoved Arlo by the shoulder. Arlo stumbled back, but kept his grip on me. I flailed and yelled around his tongue, although I doubted anyone understood me. Mostly I said variations of 'get off me' mixed with some swear words.

"Let her go," Kristos reached for me, his face dark with anger.

Arlo broke our kiss and shoved me behind him and then propelled us in tandem toward the door. "She's mine by rights."

Ah. So this was his true agenda. Well, screw that. "No I'm not. I don't belong to anyone," I shouted, twisting in his grip hoping to find a weak spot.

Arlo squeezed my wrists in warning. "Hush, tesoro. You know not of what you speak."

A jumble of images that didn't belong to me rushed through my mind, strong as a gale wind. Arlo being overrun by children under the amused watch of a woman wearing medieval clothing. More domestic scenes played out and I realized he was in my head and thinking of his long ago human family. His thoughts of me were terrifying. He wanted to breed me just like he'd said the council did, not protect me like he'd promised. Arlo wanted to try and make a family to replace the one he'd lost. The joy he felt at the prospect was blinding.

"Get out of my head," I snarled. I punched him in the back, but he didn't feel it. We were almost to the door now. If something didn't happen soon, I was about to be kidnapped and worse.

I made eye contact with Kristos who had followed us across the room and silently pleaded with him to do something. He gave a grim nod and raised his gun. "Let her go Arlo or I'll shoot."

Arlo laughed, a cold sound. "You think you can shoot fast enough? Or how about I do this?" He thrust me in front of him. "You wouldn't risk hurting her."

That made Kristos pause and the gun wavered. He didn't think he could make the shot. I put everything I had into trying to break free. I tried going limp. I jumped up and slammed my entire body weight down. I writhed like a snake. Nothing happened other than he shifted his weight a bit to compensate for the changes in mine. *Damn it.*

"Be still, Myra," Kristos said, his gaze urging me to comply.

I sagged in Arlos' arms and tried not to move. Kristos' eyes narrowed as he took the shot.

The discharge in such close quarters clobbered my

eardrums like sledgehammers. I screamed and closed my eyes waiting for the searing pain I imagined being shot would cause. Behind me I felt the force of the bullet push Arlo back. His grip slid off me as he fell to the floor with a soft grunt.

I stepped away and whirled around to see the bullet had tagged him on the shoulder. Kristos didn't waste any time making sure Arlo stayed down. The second I was clear, he was there, pressing the barrel of his gun over Arlo's heart and pulling the trigger. Arlo jumped and shuddered as the bullet tore through him, but after that he was still.

"Is he dead?" I wrapped my arms around myself to hide how badly my hands were shaking. The position served a dual purpose, allowing me to rub my incessantly itchy palm over the rough skin of my elbow. The stitches were driving me nuts.

Kristos came over to me. "No, just incapacitated. It'll take him some time to heal. Are you okay?"

"We swapped blood. He nicked his tongue in my mouth." I said with a shiver. "When you and I did that you said we were blood bound. Am I linked to him now like I was to you?" The idea terrified me.

In response to my question, Kristos waved one of his men over. "The head."

The man nodded and went over to the vampire. With business-like efficiency and enormous strength he ripped Arlo's head off. Blood so dark it was almost black sprayed everywhere in a macabre Jackson Pollack pattern.

My stomach seized up. When the guy tossed the head into the living room like we were playing a fun game of bowling, I threw up. The sight of spine and raw flesh was too much for me.

"Was that really necessary?" I asked, fighting not to vomit for a second time. The metallic scent of Arlo's blood was getting to me. I had tasted that blood. It was *in* me. Not a happy thought.

"It's the only way to break the blood bond." Kristos seemed calm and unaffected. Just another day at the office for him, I guess.

"I want a gun," I said abandoning further discussion over Arlo. I wasn't sure yet how I felt about what had happened. On one hand, he was the closest thing to family I had on my father's side. On the other, he'd wanted to rape me until I had his babies.

Kristos' gaze was cool against mine. "You ever shoot before?"

I shook my head. "No, but I'll learn. I need to be able to defend myself."

He pursed his lips. "You'll need training."

I arched an eyebrow. "Do I have time for that? I need a gun like yesterday."

"Here." He held out his, butt first. Gesturing toward Arlo's body, he said, "Shoot him."

I took the gun. It was heavier than it looked. Biting my lip, I aimed it at the headless body leisurely propped up against the wall as if certain its head would return any second now. My fingers shaking, I pulled the trigger. The gun boomed, my arm flew up and the bullet destroyed the drywall several feet above my intended target.

Kristos came to stand next to me and he unwrapped my hand to resume possession of the gun. "It's not as easy as it looks."

I shrugged. "No, but at point blank range it's harder to miss." I thought of how close I'd been to Arlo. A gun would've given us a different ending, maybe prevented the blood bond in the first place.

He tucked the gun into the waistband of his pants. "I don't want you to be defenseless, but a gun right now is asking for trouble. You don't know how to aim or how to compensate for the kickback."

I started to protest, but he held up a hand. "I'll arrange for some training, but until then, I'll be your gun."

I jutted my chin out and glared at him. "And what if you're not there?"

He held up his hands in defeat. "If I give you a different weapon, would that make you happy?"

"What kind of weapon?" I couldn't think of any useful weapons aside from a gun.

"Something easy to hide and very dangerous at point blank range."

I crossed my arms, skeptical of his offer. "Please tell me you're not giving me a wooden stake. I am not a vampire slayer." There were some slayers out there. It was a fringe lifestyle that no one took seriously and most of them died before the age of thirty.

"No, not a wooden stake." Kristos paused to chuckle at the idea. "It's a special weapon. I think you'll like it and it has deadly accuracy."

I started to speak but he cut me off. "Later. Right now, we need to leave. If anyone heard the gunshots, the police will be coming and we don't want to be here. Go make sure all your stuff is packed. We're out of here in two minutes."

I wanted to argue, but Kristos was right, this wasn't the time. Whatever weapon he had in mind for me could wait. I went into our bedroom and scanned it to be sure none of my clothes had been left behind. Finding the closet and dresser empty, I checked the bathroom, which had been cleaned out as well. Vampires apparently excelled at speed packing a suitcase.

For my part, I excelled at hyperventilating. I had to sit on the edge of the bed for a while and try to catch my breath as the images of Arlo's detached head played in my mind like a horror gif. There was too much blood in my life. And bullets. I wasn't an action adventure heroine, I was a college student trying to help her sick mom. How had things gotten so complicated and how did I make it stop?

I squeezed my eyes shut and thought as hard as I could. No answers came to me. The only thing I could do was run.

11

We traveled to Brooklyn by taxi. Kristos had turned his car over to his men instructing them to lay fake trails for anyone looking for us or Arlo. Before we'd left the apartment, Kristos had set it on fire and we left in a wail of fire alarms. While unfortunately destructive, Kristos had assured me it was the quickest way to wipe the apartment clean. The fact he had all the stuff on hand and knew how to do it gave me pause. Something told me this was not Kristos' first vampire rodeo.

Our new home wasn't as nice as the last one, which hadn't been as nice as the first one. It was a rundown brownstone. It didn't belong to Kristos, that much I could tell. The decor screamed single woman. Stacks of romance novels filled the one bookcase and where Kristos preferred coolly modern design, the brownstone had a distinct shabby chic flair. Shabby chic being code for 'picked up off the curb on garbage day.'

Despite the decor's ratty appearance, the color palette was pleasant enough; soft gray and peach with dashes of blue on the walls. The wooden furniture was nicked and scarred and the couch and chairs were clean, but slumped. Still, even if the battered leather sofa had almost taken a detour to the dump, it was comfortable.

I curled up on the sofa and pulled a blanket around my shoulders. It was fleece, one of those no-sew blankets. My mom had made a few for her chemo treatments. Cancer patients were always cold and amassed an impressive array of gloves, blankets and thick socks as a result. I didn't have cancer, but I was cold anyway. I couldn't stop seeing Arlo's head being twisted off every time I closed my eyes. *Gross.*

Kristos shoved a glass in my hand. I lifted it up and examined the amber liquid swirling inside. A spicy scent wafted up to my nose. "What is this?"

He sat next to me. "Whiskey."

I made a face.

Kristos smiled, amused. "Drink. You're too pale. This will help."

I raised my eyebrows. "You sure about that?"

He nodded and held up a little first aid kit. "It'll also numb you enough for me to take out your stitches. I noticed they've been bothering you lately."

I lifted the glass in a silent salute and then tossed it down. I sputtered as my throat spontaneously combusted. Shoving the glass at him, I wiped my mouth. "Wow."

He took the glass and set it on the coffee table. "Yeah, it's potent." Producing a small pair of scissors from the first aid kit he carefully snipped the stitches and pulled the thread free.

"Like fire in a bottle. Gah." I kept swallowing even though my mouth was empty, trying to force the burn further down my throat. I wasn't numb so much as distracted by the scorpion sting of the whiskey. Getting the stitches out didn't hurt at all by comparison, although there was an unpleasant pinching sensation as he tugged on the thread to loosen it enough to be cut.

Kristos pulled the last stitch out and released my hand. Nodding toward my glass he asked, "Do you want some more?"

I inspected my palm, relieved to see it wasn't bleeding. There would be a scar, I didn't think I could avoid one, but it was healing. Even better, with the stitches out it didn't itch so much. "No thanks. I prefer having a nervous breakdown. It stings less." I gestured to the living room. "Where are we?"

"This is the home of a friend of mine. She's away on a trip and I have a key." Kristos took my hand in his again and wrapped some sterile gauze around the wound, securing it in place with tape.

Where he found everything I didn't know. Either he had the first aid kit stashed in his bag somewhere or he knew where everything was in our new digs. Which implied he'd spent some time here. Serious time. The location of a first aid kit is not usually something you learn from casual social contact.

I gave him a look, my mind jumping to the only logical conclusion. "She? You have a key?"

Kristos tried not to look guilty and failed. "We've known each other for years."

"Like you and I know each other?" The idea rankled.

"Years ago, yes, she was my courtesan, but now we are just friends."

"Okay." I stared at the ceiling for a second as I mastered my emotions. The jealousy I felt at the idea of Kristos having other lovers surprised me. I was growing quite attached to my vampire. Yes, I thought of him as my vampire.

"Are you all right?" He laid a hand on my leg and rubbed. A little frisson of pleasure went through me at the contact.

"Just trying to compartmentalize. There's a lot going on." I took a deep breath and met his eyes. Immediately I felt like I was weightless and falling. He was using his vampire super powers on me. I looked away. "Don't do that."

"Do what?"

I gestured to his face, keeping my eyes averted. "Own me with your eyes."

"Sorry. I didn't realize I was doing it."

Oh great. The vampire super gaze was on the loose. Hide the women and children. "Whatever. So tell me what the plan is."

"I've put things in motion and we'll be on the move by tomorrow."

"What things are in motion?" I picked some lint off the fleece blanket and let it drift to the floor.

"The kind of things that will make people stop looking for

you."

"You're not going to tell me, are you?" I glared at him.

He shook his head. "This way you can't tell anyone."

"I would never tell anyone. I'm not stupid."

Now it was his turn to give me a look.

I gave a sigh of aggravation. "Okay, I shouldn't have used my ATM card or gone to the coffee shop. I've learned my lesson though, it won't happen again."

"Regardless, it's just safer if you don't know what's going to happen next." He pointed to his face. "I don't want any other vampire eyes catching you and tripping us up."

Well, that makes sense, I thought grudgingly. "I guess I have no choice."

He slipped an arm behind me and pulled me onto his lap like I was a little throw pillow. My legs spread to straddle his thighs, my knees digging into the sofa cushions. I put my hands on his shoulders to steady myself. My heart began to race with anticipation.

Kristos gripped the fullness of my backside and claimed my lips, his tongue flickering into my mouth. I moaned. My body started the launch sequence; moist heat pooled in my core, my nipples hardened inside my bra and a ceaseless want made my hips circle.

"Is this such a good idea?" I asked when he let me come up for air. Getting naked seemed risky given our circumstances. Every place we'd been, they'd found us. "Shouldn't we be on watch or something? Like a stake out?"

Kristos laughed. "You want to sleep in a car and pee in a coffee cup?"

I smacked his shoulder, but couldn't keep from smiling. "That's not what I meant and you know it."

Kristos reined in his grin and tried to look serious. "I've got it covered. The last text I got said they'd laid three different false leads and that was keeping the Council busy. We're not just hiding now, we're giving them something to chase, too."

"Give them more leads." When he quirked an eyebrow at me, I said, "Bury them with bullshit. Too much data and they won't know where to start."

"Not a bad idea, Miss Danson. You're pretty smart for only being in your twenties."

"And you're pretty hot for being dead..." I trailed off, realizing I didn't know how old he was. "How many years has it been?"

"More than I care to count." He leaned in to kiss me again, but I evaded him.

"How many?" I did my best to mimic his vampire super powers and pin him down with my gaze.

"Hundreds." He slipped with his eyes again and it seemed as if the weight of all that time was pressing against me, trying to cave me in.

I shivered and shook it off as I broke eye contact.

"Sorry," he said, apologizing before I could complain.

"Can you do that to anyone?"

He lifted his head so his eyes were focused on the ceiling. "Most humans are susceptible, but you and I are blood bound, the barriers are lower."

With a shudder, I recalled the way Arlo had blood bound me. I would not want to find myself lost in *his* eyes. Him being in my head had been bad enough. I still felt sick about it. "I can't stop you, can I?"

"Just try not to look so much into my eyes. I can't capture you if I can't see you."

While good advice, that was easier said than done. To prove the point we both moved at the same time and our gazes crossed. I sighed and looked away. "What about making me do things? Can you force me to rob a bank?"

He shook his head. "Only if we maintain eye contact which means I would have to rob the bank too. It's not like the movies where I say something and you do it even when I'm not there. We have to be able to see each other."

Well, that was a relief and something I'd been secretly worried about. "If I become a vampire, will I be able to do the eye voodoo thing to you?"

"Eye voodoo?" He cocked his head to the side at my choice of words. "No, I'll be your maker. You're never stronger than your maker."

Hmm. A hierarchy of power. "I need to be strong though, don't I?" I had a feeling that even if I turned, the attacks wouldn't stop. I was too juicy a pawn to be allowed to sink into oblivion. Too many vampires would want to find out how well I took after my dad. If I turned, at least I would be as strong as them. Staying human meant staying weak. After all, I couldn't twist off anyone's head with my bare hands, and until I could, I was ripe for the taking.

"Yes. However, if my plan works you won't have to worry about it. At least for a while." He paused for a moment and then asked, "Do you want me to turn you Myra?"

I sighed. "I don't know. I'm scared Kristos. Just last week I was a college student and I thought my biggest problem was my mom might die of cancer. Imagine the shock of learning that is the least of my problems."

I met his eyes and found him watching me with a steady gaze. The power he held over me pulsed between us like a heartbeat. I should've been more careful, but I wasn't worried about him as much as the magic eyeballs of the other vampires out there. "Why are you doing all this for me? You barely know me." Right now he was everything to me... protector *and* lover. My life without him would be over, but he didn't need me.

"Myra." His hands pressed on my back, pushing me forward for a kiss. This time he would not be denied. Our tongues dueled and his teeth scraped my bottom lip as he sucked it into his mouth. "Because you're special," he finally said once he'd had his fill of my mouth.

"You want me like Arlo did." My tone was accusatory. I

leaned back and crossed my arms.

Kristos tugged at my wrists, trying to unwrap me and force me to open for him. "Every vampire wants you, but you're not a pawn to me. You're too special for that. I want you for you."

"Really?" I asked in a soft whisper.

"I promise you, Myra. You are more than your father's blood to me."

"Swear it," I said.

He held up a hand, his expression solemn. "By our blood bond, I swear it."

We stopped talking for a long moment to kiss again. Kristos cradled the back of my head and pressed me forward as he devoured my lips with his. His tongue slipped into the wet heat of my mouth, stroking the length of mine and sending little shocks through me.

He pulled back for a second. "Tell me Myra, why do you stay with me? Why don't you run?"

The questions surprised me. "Because you're my only protection. You're taking care of my mom."

A disappointment I didn't understand shone in his eyes. "That's all?"

I cupped his face in my hands wanting to make it better. I'd hurt him somehow. "Every cell of my being wants you. All the time. It is unceasing. I've never felt that way before and..." I trailed off.

He gave my ass a little squeeze at the silence. "And what?"

"You were my first." I blushed. "That makes *you* special. I don't want to be with anyone else."

As usual the red flush drove him crazy and he seized my mouth with his, kissing me so fiercely I ran out of air. When he let me go, my breathing came in ragged pants and my lungs burned. Desire ran hot underneath my skin. I wanted him, *now.* I moved to lift my shirt over my head, but Kristos stopped me.

"You surprise and delight me constantly and that is a hard thing to do. I know the circumstances are not ideal, but I am glad we are together. You make me feel my heart again."

The flush burning my cheeks and neck intensified. "You are entirely too nice to be a vampire."

"No, I'm only nice to you." With that, he pulled my shirt off and unhooked my bra, moving so fast my eyes could barely keep up with him. More vampire super powers. I liked it this time, though, and thrust my chest out as he cupped my breasts in his hands.

Dipping his head, he sucked one nipple and lightly pinched the other. The firm pressure carried just enough edge to make my core clench with need. Smiling wickedly around my breast he tugged the other nipple out and forward, stretching and pinching at the same time. I rewarded him with a deep moan.

Supporting my back with his hands he half stood and laid me on the pine coffee table, clearing the surface with a swipe of his hand. Magazines and the whiskey glass fell to the floor. He unbuttoned my jeans and inched them off my hips, hands grazing my skin and raising goose bumps. I thrust my pelvis up at him, a silent request to go faster, which he did. With one quick pull, my pants were off and tossed onto the couch. My panties he just ripped, the sheer lace giving way like tissue paper.

He pushed one, then two insistent fingers inside me as his thumb found the sensitive nub between my nether lips. I threw my head back and sighed.

"You like that, love?"

"Very much," I breathed.

And then he crooked his fingers within me, pushing into overly sensitive flesh. I gasped as a small burst of fireworks went off in my core. The pressure of a larger explosion began to build and I gripped the edge of the table.

"Kristos," I keened.

"Yes, love I'm here." His hand went faster, harder. My hips bounced, racing toward the cliff. I sailed right off into weightless pleasure. I couldn't breathe or think. My eyes closed putting me in a dark place where trembling sensation was all that mattered.

Still lost in the orgasm, I felt the faint pin-pricks of fangs on my inner thigh. That sent another tremor through me as my body responded with heightened pleasure. Kristos' lips sealed over the hyper-sensitive skin of my leg and milked me with measured contractions of his mouth. I couldn't stay still. It tickled and I writhed and wriggled until he had to hold me down.

The orgasm continued to shiver through me, pulsing in time with Kristos' mouth on my thigh. I wondered if it was some kind of vampire pheromone thing that caused him to have such an effect on me. Or maybe it was the blood bond. I would have to ask him sometime.

Having had his fill of me, he impaled me on his shaft. Scooting his hands under my shoulder blades, he lifted me into a sitting position and transferred us both to the couch.

"Oh," I breathed at the change in sensation. He went so much deeper in me now and his pelvis split my nether lips wide to rub against my delicate center. It was very satisfying.

Kristos reached around to squeeze my rear and when I slid down his length, he gave me an extra push, ensuring I took all of him in and then some. He captured a nipple in his mouth and sucked it in long pulls. His tongue flickered over the tip until the fluttering sensation spread all through my body. After a moment, he switched breasts and gave the other the same treatment.

All I could do was pump along his shaft and pant as desire consumed me.

When I came again, he pulled me in close. My pebbled breasts hit his chest as he thrust his tongue into my mouth. I tasted blood again and recoiled in surprise, but he wove his fingers into my hair and forced me to maintain the kiss. The last time he'd kissed me like this, I'd almost thrown up. The sour iron of blood had been unpleasant, but necessary. Now, the flavor was like a full bodied wine, the tang almost fruity as opposed to metallic. I found myself enjoying his blood, even relishing it as it slipped down my throat. I began to see the connection with alcohol that had so puzzled me when I first met Madame Rouge.

My eyes opened and sought his, which were their usual crystalline blue with the force of a tsunami behind them. He drank me in and my mind rolled over under the force of his eyes. He didn't speak, but it seemed I could hear him in my head anyway.

Suck, love.

Take as much of me as you can.

I obeyed, earnestly working his tongue. Inside me his cock pulsed and danced. He came a moment later and broke our kiss to sink his fangs into my neck. Once again a little spasm of pleasure shook me as he fed. I continued to pump his shaft, lost in a blissful stupor.

Afterward we retired to the bedroom. Here the shabby chic decor had morphed into country farmhouse with an old-fashioned four post bed and a pair of vintage oak dressers. The patchwork quilt lent the room color and there were touches of lace on the night tables and in the large doilies on top of the dressers. The look was discordant given the apartment's location in one of the largest metropolis' in the world, however, I found it comforting. I'd grown up in rooms furnished like this. It was like being home again.

I sank into the bed, snuggling under the covers, sated both in body and mind. Kristos had drained me of blood and energy. A lethargy of deep satisfaction made me limp and ready to sleep.

Kristos spooned me, his unyielding strength at my back reassuring. With one hand he spun little circles on my shoulder. I wiggled my bottom against him and sighed. Just then all my troubles seemed far, far away. All that mattered was the here and now.

"How did you become a vampire?" I wanted to hear his voice as I drifted off.

His fingers on my shoulder stilled. "It's a long story. An unpleasant history."

"Worse than ripping off Arlo's head?" I asked, my question pointed.

That gave him pause. "Perhaps not." He was silent for a moment, fingers idling on my skin. "I lived in Rome during the time of Cleopatra and Julius Caesar."

That sparked my interest. "Did you know them?"

"Only when they passed through the main streets on their way to the palace. I did not run in their circles."

"So you weren't a Senator in ancient Rome." I managed not to sound too disappointed. The idea of being with a guy who'd met Cleopatra held a certain allure.

"No. My family ran a bakery."

I frowned. A bakery seemed so mundane. "How did you go from bread to blood?"

"I met a man in the baths. In those days men often had boy lovers. A powerful vampire chose me to be his. He was compelling and strangely beautiful in a time when many men of power were disfigured somehow, either from disease or war. He seduced me and then years later turned me to keep me as his pet."

"How did you feel about that?" I half-turned to look at him, but he didn't seem to notice. He was gazing into the distance, lost in another time, another place.

"At first I was angry. I missed my family and felt like my future had been stolen from me. I would spare you this bitterness if I could." He gave my shoulder a gentle squeeze. "Still, I am not so unhappy now. I have seen such miracles, lived to see one era fade into the next and now technology will bring us to the heights of gods. Drinking blood seems a small price to pay."

"Drinking blood is not the only cost, is it?" I asked thinking of the non-stop violence that had ensued since we'd met. "Do vampires always go around playing shoot 'em up and ripping off heads?"

Kristos went still again. "We have our moments, yes. Mostly we coexist peacefully, especially in the modern era, but you will bring out the worst in us, Myra."

"There's one thing I don't get." I rolled over to face him. "How did they know about me? I think I understand why vampires want me, but how did they find me?" I'd gone twenty-five years without a peep and then all hell had broken loose.

Kristos didn't meet my eyes for once. "In one word, it's genetics. Vampires want to make better vampires. You do that by finding and turning descendants of powerful vampires. Cousins or surviving children's children are believed to have the potential to be stronger than others of our kind. Someone must have seen Devon's name on the birth certificate."

"That simple?"

He nodded. "That simple. Some vampires want to bring over their families for sentimental reasons. Others are more mercenary about building a power base. Someone found out about you."

"Do you think it's because I became a blood courtesan? Madame Rouge had enough information to do a background check."

He shrugged. "That's possible. Or maybe you just came up on a search. I've known vampires who actively collected humans that had the same DNA as a powerful vampire."

I made a face at the idea of being stalked for my genetic material. "Could it be my dad looking for me?" Was he still out there somewhere? Would I ever meet him?

"I suppose, but Devon's been gone for so long you should prepare yourself for the idea that he's met his final death." He wrapped his arms around me again and pulled me close. "Now rest, love. Tomorrow night will be busy and we don't want to be fatigued."

"Kristos?"

"Rest, Myra," he chided.

"Just one more question." I twisted around to look at him. "Where is your maker now?"

A shadow crossed his face. "He died the final death."

I cupped his cheek in my hand. "I'm sorry."

He gave a little shrug and despite the shadow that crossed

his face, he said, "It was a long time ago."

We shared a companionable silence after that. Kristos pulled me tight against him and buried his face in the nape of my neck as if seeking comfort. I leaned into him wanting to give him what solace I could, and before I knew it, I was asleep.

12

I slept until early afternoon the next day. My stomach woke me, growling and wanting to be fed. Grumbling about my incessant need to eat, I used the bathroom and then poked around in the meager kitchen. Locating some bread, butter and jam I made toast.

As I ate, I went through the owner's mail, which was piled on the kitchen counter. Her name was Charlene Townsend and she got a lot of catalogs. I set those aside to look at later and flipped through her bills out of idle curiosity about the woman who had slept with Kristos before me. A large manila envelope rested at the bottom of the pile and when I found it already open, I pulled out the contents which turned out to be several news clippings.

I scanned them recognizing the name Townsend. The clippings were old, dating back to the nineteen fifties, and checking the envelope again, I found copies of news stories from the eighteen hundreds.

None of the stories were all that interesting. One from 1880 talked about someone named Charles Townsend who'd bought some land and built a school house for a small town in rural Georgia. They were so grateful the newspaper did a full write up, droning on and on and on about the man like he was some saint. They covered his parents, where they grew up, where he grew up, his schooling and his marital status. There was also a picture of him standing in front of what looked to be a one room schoolhouse constructed of clapboard. He was a weird looking guy with a lean, tall face and one of those old-timey square beards.

I set everything down for a second to put more bread in the toaster. While it toasted, I gathered up all the clippings intent on putting them back in the envelope, but one of the articles caught my eye. This one was an actual newspaper clipping from 1959. The picture it contained stopped me short. It was of a man who looked a lot like the Charles Townsend of 1880. The beard had disappeared, but he hadn't aged one bit.

Curious, I pulled out the 1880 piece again and compared the two pictures as a shiver went up my spine. My conversation with Kristos came back to me. If this Charles Townsend was a vampire back then, he was probably related to Charlene. Was she on some kind of DNA hit list too? Was she on the run just like me?

I put the clippings back in the envelope and tried to arrange the mail to look natural, like no one had been combing through it. A red folder then caught my attention. It hadn't been in the mail pile but off to the side. I flipped it open and my jaw dropped as I read the letter on top.

Mr. Townsend:

My name is Charlene and we're distant cousins, related on your mother's side. I would like to meet with you to discuss our family.

Something you may not know is we have a gene that makes us prone to cancer. It killed my mother, her mother, and both my sisters. It stretches generations back in our family tree. As far as I can tell, cancer killed your own mother. Myself, I already have some early cell changes that indicate the beginning stages of cancer.

I don't want to die like the other women in my family and you are my only option. I want to live and I'll do anything I have to in order to do so.

I stopped reading at that point as the letter went on to give contact information that didn't interest me. Returning the letter to its folder, I riffled through the other papers inside, which consisted of dull genealogy research. Charlene had done her homework. Nothing interesting came to light, so I set the folder back on the counter.

My mind whirled. I didn't blame Charlene at all for taking such a drastic step. Maybe it was something I should consider for myself. Up until then I'd thought the whole 'to be or not to be a bloodsucker' debate was about keeping me safe from my attackers, but what if I had the same genes Charlene did?

I blinked and the image of my emaciated grandmother lying in a hospital bed came to mind. She'd lasted a month after her diagnosis. Cancer was hell on earth. Even the kind they could cure was no picnic. Shoot, if I'd known about my father before, I might've approached him on my mother's behalf. Becoming a vampire couldn't be worse than failed chemo, right?

Disconcerted by Charlene and the questions her situation raised for me, I busied myself with making even more toast—hey, I was hungry. Wanting to distract myself, I took the catalogs to the couch and indulged in some fantasy retail while munching on the toast. Charlene got some nice catalogs; she was clearly in a much higher income bracket than me.

An hour later found me restlessly roaming the apartment. It was hours until dark. The catalogs hadn't lasted for long and there was nothing on TV but sappy soap operas, PBS kid shows and Judge Judy. Charlene didn't have extended cable. I wanted to call my mom, but Kristos had confiscated my cell phone saying something about vampires monitoring and tracing calls. For ancient myths, they were pretty up with the times.

When I spotted an old-school button phone by the front door, I couldn't resist the temptation. Surely they wouldn't be tracking such old technology? My mom was under an assumed name anyway. There was nothing linking us and I needed to hear her voice.

I lifted the receiver and smiled when I heard a dial tone. After a good fifteen minutes of calling information and making my way through department after department, I finally reached my mom.

"Honey!" Her voice was breezy and carefree. She sounded thrilled to hear from me.

"Mom," I said. "How are things going?" It was so good to hear her voice. Even with my life in danger, there was always background worry about my mom. Was she safe? How was her cancer? Would she live?

"I'm doing great. I'm in a new drug trial and it's working really well. I might be done next week."

"That's great, mom." The news eased my worries somewhat. As CEO of a large conglomerate with medical interests, Kristos had been able to pull some serious strings at his company to arrange cutting-edge medical care for my mom. Thanks to him, she had a better chance than ever at surviving cancer.

"How are you doing? Did everything work out with the internship?"

I winced at the reminder of my lie. "Yeah. It looks like I got the job," I said. Given that I didn't know when this would be all over it was probably a good idea to let her think I was occupied with a high powered internship.

"That's fantastic. I'll have to come to the city and see you once I have the all clear."

"Sure, that would be great." I paused, hesitating over what I was about to say next. "Hey mom, what can you tell me about my dad?" I held my breath waiting for her response. It was a long shot—we'd never talked much about him—but maybe she could shed some light on things.

"I was only with him that one night. I'm not proud of that, Myra, and I don't recommend it, but I guess I got swept up in the moment. Your father was very charismatic. He had the most beautiful eyes." Her voice grew distant as her memories came to the fore.

I grimaced at the mention of eyes. It sounded like falling under a vampire's spell ran in the family. "You never saw him again?"

"No. I looked for him when I found out I was pregnant, but it was like he never existed. I put his name on your birth certificate hoping he would come find us someday. Why do you ask?"

I twisted the phone cord around my hand, unsure of how much to say. We'd managed to keep the fact that she'd been kidnapped by vampires from her, for her sake as much as mine. As far as she knew, some whacko had snatched her and we had tracked her down. She had yet to notice there'd been no police or question why she woke up in Kristos' bed. Being hit on the head and possibly drugged has its good points, I guess.

"Honey?" my mom prompted concerned by my long silence.

I gave myself a little shake. "Sorry, it's just that I met someone who might've known him. Just curious, that's all."

"Oh, do tell?" Excitement brightened her voice.

"I will, but later. I have to go right now. My boss is waiting for me," I said with as much conviction as I could muster. Lying to my mom didn't feel good, but I was nowhere near ready to discuss the truth and I doubted she was ready to hear it. "Call you later?"

"All right, honey. Take care of yourself. Love you."

"Love you too, mom." I hung up and stared at the receiver. I wanted to cry. Everything was such a mess.

"Evening," said Kristos.

I jumped at the sound of his voice and turned to find him standing practically right next to me wearing just a loose pair of pajama pants. Had he been listening the whole time? I looked to the bay window at the front of the living room, noting the creeping shadows of dusk. "You're up."

"And you're getting into trouble as usual." He gestured to the phone. "It's not safe to call her right now."

I stood up and faced him. "I thought you just meant on my cell phone." Annoyance flashed through me. "Besides, she's my mom and she's sick. I have to stay in touch."

He crossed his arms over his bare chest and leveled a stern gaze at me. I met it, unflinching and ready to fight.

"Why don't you change my mom?" I asked.

The question surprised him and he raised his eyebrows. "Myra,"

"I mean, it would stop the cancer right?" It made sense for Charlene so why not my mom?

Kristos gripped my shoulders. "Myra," he said again, in a soft soothing voice. The kind of tone people use to break bad news. "She's sick and weak. Turning her could kill her."

I shrugged off his hands. "If she gets better? If she goes

into remission?"

He tilted his head and looked at me. "Maybe."

"Maybe?" My voice went up an octave. "Isn't the whole point to raise someone from the dead?"

Kristos frowned. "Cancer isn't like other mortal wounds. It eats you from the inside. I can raise a man who's been shot or stabbed. The loss of blood can be overcome, although even then it can be risky. Cancer rots you from within and can lead to a diseased vampire. Even if someone can be raised, not everyone should be."

Thinking of Charlene I asked, "What if you only have a few active cancer cells? If you've caught it early?"

He looked thoughtful. "I don't know. It's not something that vampires have worried about. I suppose given how prevalent pre-cancerous cell mutations are that it's possible people have been turned in the early stages. As far as knowing that and following what happened next?" He shook his head. "It hasn't been done."

"But if you could turn her, you would, right?"

Kristos pursed his lips. He didn't like my question. "Myra—"

"It's a yes or no question." I crossed my arms and glared at him. "How could you be so quick to change me and not my mom?"

"Because you're one of us, she's not. Does she even want to be a vampire? Believe it or not, some people don't welcome this life. I don't see you lining up to claim your heritage." At that last statement he hit me with the full force of his gaze. My knees threatened to buckle, but I held firm through sheer force of will.

The truth of what he said warred with what I wanted. For myself. For my mom.

He raised his hands in a placating gesture. "Listen, no decision has to be made now. How about we see what happens? Would that be enough for you?" His tone was pleading. He didn't want to fight. Not about this.

We stared at each other in silence, tension bristling between us, until with a sigh I nodded. I didn't want to fight about it either, not when I couldn't even make the decision to become a vampire for myself.

Kristos smiled at me, half in apology, half in an attempt to lighten the mood. "Did a package arrive today?"

I shook my head."Not that I know of."

Kristos went to the front door and opened it to reveal a brown box on the welcome mat.

Its appearance irritated me. "So you can give out our location but I can't call my mom? What's that about?" I crossed my arms and glared at him, suddenly angry with him again.

"Experience. I know what I'm doing." Kristos said, his voice flat. He took the box into the kitchen and opened it using his super fang strength to rip through the packaging tape.

I wanted to argue with him further, but what he pulled from the box rendered me speechless. It was a gleaming silver dagger about as long as my forearm with a very sharp point on the end. "What is that?"

"The weapon I promised you." He handed me the dagger, hilt first, and rummaged in the box until he found a sheath and a silver flask.

I waved the dagger in the air finding it lighter than I expected. The blade was not flat, but slightly rounded as if it there was something inside. Finding a small button on top of the hilt, I pushed it and gasped when a series of small holes appeared at the end of the blade, just behind the tip. "What the hell?" I gaped at the holes, confused. "You gave me a hollow knife?" I glared at him.

Kristos found my reaction amusing and smiled. Holding up the flask he said, "It's hollow to hold this."

My eyes narrowed. "This being?"

"Holy water. It's like acid to vampires. It won't kill us, but it will render us harmless for a time." He pointed to his eye. "I suggest stabbing your victim through here and melting their brain with the holy water. Even the undead need a central nervous system and if you destroy that, they won't be able to move until it regenerates."

I made a face. "That's disgusting."

"But effective." He handed me the sheath. "This will fit around your calf under your clothes or around your thigh over your pants."

I took the sheath and strapped it around my thigh. Putting the dagger inside, I walked around the living room to test it out. "How do I carry the flask?" The sheath would only hold the knife.

Kristos hooked a finger in the belt loop of my waistband

and pulled me close. One hand went down to cup my ass, while the other tucked the flask down my jeans at the small of my back. Then he took the dagger and showed me how to unscrew the top. "You fill it in here." He handed me the two pieces. "You put it back together. It's your weapon, you should know how to use it."

I pulled the flask out and filled the dagger as Kristos watched. Once it was reassembled I returned the dagger to its sheath and tucked the flask back against my tailbone.

"If you're careful, you should be able to get three vampires without refilling. Don't hold the button down too long or you'll waste the holy water."

"You seem to know a lot about killing vampires, Kristos." To me he was a lover, not a fighter. His colder, more mercenary side always caught me by surprise. It was easier for me to remember the sex and forget the rest.

He shrugged. "We have fought our wars. Vampires can be predatory, not just with humans, but amongst ourselves."

"I've noticed," I said dryly.

"Before guns we had weapons like this dagger. Slayers designed it sometime around the Spanish Inquisition and we copied them."

"You ever use a wooden stake?"

He grimaced. "No. It's like trying to pierce stone with a toothpick. The stake is overrated by slayers. It takes them years to perfect their aim and build the strength to penetrate the ribcage through to the heart. There are better ways to go about it."

I shivered. "Such as beheading." God, I wished I could get Arlo's death out of my head, but it haunted me like my own personal ghost.

He nodded. "Yes and there are better weapons than a stake."

"Like a bow and arrow?" I asked.

That made him wince. "Yes. Although, I would prefer it if you didn't go around announcing that. We like the slayers' antiquated doctrine just the way it is, for everyone's sakes. If they abandon their traditionalism and modernize their approach to killing vampires, it will be war."

"I think you should turn me," I said, changing the subject.

He looked at me with a surprised expression. "What brought this on?"

"I'm not strong enough, Kristos." I had a weapon now, true, but I still felt exposed and outgunned. Our earlier conversation had given me some food for thought as well. I had been dragging my feet, unsure of what I wanted, but I knew that needed to change.

Kristos wrapped me in his arms. "But I am strong enough for both of us, love. You don't have to decide now."

"I feel like I'm running out of time." I leaned my forehead against his chest, taking comfort in his steady strength.

"After tonight we'll have all the time in the world." He kissed the top of my head. "There's no need to rush anything."

"Promise?" I asked in a small voice. Were there really

dates with Kristos in my future that didn't involve heavy artillery?

"Promise." He inhaled. "You smell wonderful. Like butter and raspberries." His grip tightened around me, pushing me into him and allowing me to feel the bulge between his legs.

"I had a lot of toast," I murmured into his pecs. "With a lot of butter and jam. There was nothing else to eat." With a pang, I recalled the bag of bakery goodies that had been left behind at the previous apartment. They were probably nothing more than charred ash now.

His hands moved down to cup my ass cheeks, grinding my pelvis into his. In response, I pressed my lips against his chest, tasting him. How was it that I wanted him again so soon? He was like an aphrodisiac that ran hot in my blood.

Kristos raised my chin and kissed me as his hands roamed my body.

"Do we have time for this?" I whispered against his mouth.

"A few moments." His lips curved on mine as he flashed a smile. "Enough to take you to my satisfaction."

Before I knew it, my jeans were unbuttoned and the dagger and flask cast aside. My shirt followed and then another pair of panties were sacrificed to passion. He sat me on the kitchen counter and his finger found the sweet spot between my legs as he nuzzled the nape of my neck.

I threw my head back and spread my legs wider to give him ample room. "At this rate I'm going to run out of underwear."

"Good," he said sounding satisfied. "I like you with fewer

clothes."

"Me too, but only when we're alone. Out there," I waved my hand at the large bay window that faced the street, "I like to wear a clean pair of underwear."

"You and your panty problems never cease to amaze me." His other hand was under my shirt, shoving my bra out of the way and plucking at my nipples in turn, feeding the ache in my belly. "If I had my way, you would be naked all the time for me."

"No clothes at all?" I arched an eyebrow at him.

"I might bind you in chains of gold. A little clamp here," he pinched the nub at my core for emphasis, "And another two up here." Kristos ran his hands across my breasts. "Just to keep your senses on high alert. Then I would tie you up while I slept so you would have nothing else to do but think about me."

My eyes widened. To my surprise, his words were titillating as opposed to repellant. I shook my head, remembering how afraid I'd been of the torture chamber in his apartment. Now I kind of liked the idea of being helpless and left to writhe for him as passion did a slow burn through my erogenous zones. It sounded hot and now I trusted Kristos enough to do something like that. Maybe we could experiment after this current mess had been settled.

"How would the clamps feel?" I asked, curious. "Would they hurt?"

"Enough to keep you on the edge." To illustrate he gave a nipple a firm pinch, digging into the flesh with his nail.

My breathing hitched and I felt a flood of wetness between my legs.

He caught the reaction and did the same to the other nipple with a wicked smile. "You were a delectable virgin, Myra, but I like your new sense of adventure even more." With that, he kneeled down and brought his face to the nexus of my core. I had to scoot off the counter so he could reach me, using my hands on the counter's edge to support myself.

Kristos licked and stroked me until I trembled. When he thrust his tongue deep inside my wet passage, my knees started to buckle and he had to hold me up, pinning me against the counter by my hips. Then he returned to the sensitive nub and worked it over until I keened with the pleasure. The orgasm swelled hot and wet inside me and then burst as he lashed my core with rapid flicks back and forth. I moaned and all strength fled my body until the only thing keeping me upright was Kristos' hands at my hips.

"How do you do this to me?" I asked. "I can never get enough of you. You're like a drug."

"It's the blood bond," he said rising to his feet and steadying me with his hands.

I leaned into him, still weak from my climax. "The second you touch me, I want you. Every time."

"And I you." He kissed me, sharing the salty flavor of my desire.

"You feel like that too?"

"Oh yes, Myra. I want you too. Any way and every way."

He lifted my shirt over my head and dropped it to the floor while I shrugged out of my bra. Then he turned me until I faced the counter, and with gentle insistence, bent me over it. "I want you always, even after we've just made love. It's unlike any other binding I've experienced." He nudged my feet apart and pressed on the small of my back into an expectant arch.

I heard him unzip his pants and then his hard length pressed between my legs. He slowly sank himself into my slick wetness with a guttural groan. I sighed in satisfaction. With Kristos inside me, I felt complete.

At first he set a slow, teasing pace that had me pushing back trying to take more of him faster. He ignored me and forced me to accept his pace, one that reduced me to begging.

"Faster, Kristos. Please."

"Not yet, love. I want to savor you."

I wiggled my hips in frustration and his hands grabbed an ass cheek each, giving me a firm squeeze until I stilled. The pleasure rose in shallow eddies as he pumped in and out of me, lacking the stimulation to crest. It felt good, oh so good, but it wasn't enough. I mewled in frustration.

Kristos ran his hand along my back pushing me down so that my ass rose up even higher for him. My chest had slipped off the counter by then and I hung onto the edge with my hands, head bent down toward the floor. It reminded me of a yoga pose except that had been awkward, and this felt so good I wanted it to hurry up and never stop at the same time.

When he stopped and pulled out, I almost cried, but he quickly helped me upright and around to set me on the counter. With one quick thrust he was inside me again and sucking my nipples, one after the other. His tongue on my breasts was impatient and merciless. He didn't feed from me, but his teeth scraped my sensitive skin anyway and I gasped at the sensation.

"You like it rough, don't you, Myra?" he asked with a knowing smile. To prove his point he took my nipple in his mouth, whipped it into a frenzy with his tongue and then bit down none-too-gently.

I yelped and put a hand to his head, threading my fingers through his hair and holding him in place so he wouldn't stop. The most delicious sensations throbbed in my body. The sweet pleasure of his cock inside me and the tortured bliss of his mouth and teeth on my breasts.

Yes, I liked it rough.

I bucked against him as I spun out of control. He started to slam into me with punishing strokes and I exploded with a scream. He came with me. Kristos wasn't one to make much noise during sex, but the way he clenched his jaw when he climaxed gave it away. That and he stopped moving inside me.

We shuddered into one another as the aftershocks of our shared pleasure rolled through us and then Kristos slowly moved away, breaking contact. I missed the feel of him against my skin immediately. I wanted to say, 'let's do that again' but instead I went to my luggage, found another pair of underwear, and got dressed.

Not wanting to wear the dagger where people could see it, I strapped the sheath around my calf and slipped the dagger inside. My tight designer jeans had just enough give in them to cover the whole thing, although you could see the shape of it through the cloth. I hoped the dark indigo blue would camouflage it enough to prevent questions. What I couldn't figure out was how I would draw the dagger without wrestling with my jeans for five minutes. Having a weapon was progress, but not being able to access it quickly made it moot.

Kristos, ever observant, silently came over with a kitchen knife. Squatting down he hacked a slit just above the sheath and wide enough for my hand to pass through. I winced as he did it, thinking of Jacques, the stylist who'd chosen my clothes back when all I had to worry about was having sex with a vampire.

Kristos returned the knife to its drawer. "Check and see if you can draw like that."

I pulled the knife out and then put it back in. "Seems fine. Although Jacques will kill me if he finds out." The stylist would have a fit. He didn't care if I lived or died, it was all about the clothes with him and I'd just committed an act of fashion blasphemy. He would never forgive me.

"Jacques is the least of your worries, love," Kristos murmured. He went into the bedroom and emerged a second later wearing a crisp white dress shirt paired with navy dress pants. Slung over his shoulder was the black leather duffel bag he used as luggage. "Ready to go, love?"

I grabbed the little rolling suitcase one of Kristos' men had bought for me when we first went into hiding. "I guess. I wish you would tell me the plan."

"You'll know soon enough," came his enigmatic response.

13

We left the Brownstone, the air now cold enough with impending winter to make my breath fog. Kristos led the way down a few blocks and then over a few more. His rapid gait made it so I had to hustle to keep up with him.

"This is not the Olympic power walking race," I said to him after I had to actually break into a run or risk being left behind at a crosswalk.

He slowed down for a moment. "Sorry. I'm just edgy." And then he sped up again, forcing me into a light jog. For a second I had a little flashback to the night we first met and the way his goons had swept me along at such a pace that I'd tripped and fallen. I grimaced at the memory, which seemed to delight in taunting me.

By the time we arrived at the subway station, my heart pounded in my ears and I was flushed and out of breath. Kristos bought two tickets and a few minutes later we were on a train destined for the Grand Central stop in Manhattan. Kristos remained silent but alert, his eyes constantly scanning the people around us. The train jostled us against each other in a not unpleasant rhythm and I watched the world stream by outside the window, trying to bite back anxiety about what would happen next.

At Grand Central, Kristos guided me out to the street and flagged a taxi. He gave the driver an address that made no sense to me and I found myself wishing I knew the terrain of New York City better. All I caught was something tower followed by a bunch of street numbers. Knowing he wouldn't tell me, I didn't ask.

Kristos leaned back in the seat next to me and reached out to squeeze my knee. "So far, so good. We're almost home free."

I opened my mouth to say something about how I couldn't wait, but before I could utter a word, a black SUV squealed around the corner at the cross street in front of us. Its engine roaring, it zeroed in on our vehicle.

The cab driver screamed. "We're going to crash. Brace yourselves!"

I looked at Kristos as I gripped the 'oh shit' handle with both hands. There was no time to do anything else before the SUV smashed into the front end of our taxi. The impact slammed me back into my seat with such force that I rebounded forward, my head hitting the plastic partition dividing the front of the taxi from the back. Pain split my skull and while my eyes were open, I couldn't see anything but darkness and weird little sparkles. Reaching out my hand I felt for Kristos, relieved when I found his shoulder.

"Myra, are you okay?" he asked, sounding surprisingly unaffected by the accident. Super vamp probably didn't have a scratch on him.

"I think so," I managed to whisper, my words slurring together like I was drunk. "My head hurts."

"I'm going to get out and come around to your side. Don't move, okay?"

I heard the sound of his car door opening and waited for him to open mine, trying to stay as still as possible because movement was painful. The cab driver groaned in his seat and a blinker clicked incessantly. I hoped the guy was okay and I really wished someone would shut off the damn blinker, it made my head hurt even more. My eyesight was beginning to clear now, revealing splashes of colors alternated with shadows. I could see parts of the taxi, but blackout spots kept my vision from being whole.

My door opened and hands grabbed me, hauling me out into the street. I looked up expecting to see Kristos, but the man above me was not him. While I was processing that fact, a gun shot rang out and someone made a loud 'oof' sound as the bullet connected. I tracked the noise and stopped breathing when I saw Kristos flat on the ground in the middle of the street, his eyes dead and staring up at nothing.

"Kristos!" I screamed, fighting to break free and go to him, but whoever had me was stronger than I would ever be. Vampire strong. The thought hit me and I went still. They'd found us and I'd just lost my only protector. My heart convulsed and tears streamed down my cheeks. Was he dead or just incapacitated? Would I ever see him again? I couldn't bear the idea of not having Kristos at my back. He'd been amazing from day one. The thought of being without him made grief close my throat, choking me on my own sobs.

I didn't even fight when the vampire dragged me away from the scene. A black limo pulled up alongside us. When the door opened, I was unceremoniously stuffed inside.

I sprawled on the floor of the limo. It took me a minute to recover because the rapid movement had sloshed my already scrambled brain. It felt like there was a huge bruise inside my skull and it throbbed in pulses of sharp agony. With a groan, I pulled myself into an empty seat and tried to take stock of my surroundings.

There were three of them sitting on the bench seat across from me. All men. All vampires. I could tell by their pallor and the lack of small movements. Vampires were still as statues when they stopped moving.

One of the trio was the guy who had grabbed me. He was built like a prizefighter with a shiny bald head, bulging arm muscles and large, ham hands that could probably wrap all the way around my neck.

The second was dressed in a meticulous three-piece suit with fancy Italian leather shoes. He had brown hair and unremarkable features. He looked like a corporate middle manager and reminded me of one of my professors in school.

The third vampire was Abe Lincoln tall, his knees rising high up past the seat level. His arms were long and thin and he wore black trousers with a black dress shirt and black shoes. The expression on his face gave me a start as he watched me with the intensity of a lion stalking its prey. His dark eyes reminded me of Arlo and made me feel like I was staring down a black hole of nothingness.

He smiled at me, his thin lips making the expression a threat full of malice. "Hello, my daughter."

14

I stared at the man across from me, taking in his narrow face and high cheek bones that were eerily similar to mine. My mouth dropped open in shock and my eyes went so wide I thought for sure they would pop out of my head. "D-d-dad?" The word sounded wrong on my tongue. This was my Dad? *Oh God I hope not.* Because that would mean my dad hadn't just missed my entire life to date, he'd also shot Kristos. My stomach clenched. This wasn't going to be a happy reunion.

His smile widened, revealing pointed fangs. "Yes, it's me, your sire." He waved to the vampires next to him. "These are my associates. Say hello to my daughter."

The two vampires gave slight nods of their heads.

Ignoring the introductions, I kept my focus on what mattered. "Kristos?" I couldn't keep myself from sounding hopeful. The idea of him gone was killing me.

At the mention of Kristos' name Devon's expression soured and his dark eyes flashed. "He will no longer trouble you, daughter. You are mine. You will always be mine." His gaze pinned me down then and I froze as the power of his eyes hit me.

Somehow he was inside my head, rummaging through it like so many dresser drawers. Arlo had invaded me with his thoughts and Kristos had been able to create a common link between us, but we had all exchanged blood. This vampire, my father, was inside my mind easy as a knife cutting butter. I had no resistance to him.

He caught my thought process and gave a satisfied smile. "You were blood bound to me at birth, dear one. I chose not to invoke it until you were old enough to be useful to me." He paused for a second and then asked, "But what is this about Arlo? You knew him?"

He poked around my memories and brought back the night I'd first met Arlo. He winced at the picture of the decapitation.

"Did you send him after me?" I asked. It took enormous effort for me to speak, the weight of him in my head was suffocating and banging my skull around like a piñata hadn't done me any favors either.

Devon shook his head. "No, I set him loose some time ago. He's no longer mine. Pity he had to die like that, but if you hadn't killed him I would have." He leaned forward and rested a long bony finger on my knee. "No one touches what's mine, daughter. No one." The pressure of his finger intensified until it dug into my thigh like a hard rock.

My spine crawled at his touch and all sorts of alarms went

off in my head. Devon may be my father but he was no doting parent. In my fantasies, I'd always imagined meeting my Dad to be a joyous moment, but in reality, I was filled with a gnawing fear. The guy was a creep.

The good thing about our conversation, Devon's focus on me had lessened. I took advantage of the lull to send out a panicky thought toward the bond I had shared with Kristos. *Are you okay? Can you feel me?* Normally I would have sensed the connection between us but this time there was only emptiness. The place in my soul that had held Kristos was vacant. My heart sank.

I was alone and my 'Dad' made an angry cobra seem safe.

Putting on a brave front, I said, "Where are we going?"

"I'm taking you home, child. Where you belong. I would have come for you sooner, but it took time to make suitable arrangements for your care." The limo lurched to a stop as he spoke and the two vampires at his side, quickly exited the vehicle. Devon motioned for me to go first and I stepped out into the frigid winter night, my feet unsteady and my spirits failing.

Devon poured out of the limo in a smooth, graceful motion. Standing, he towered over everyone, confirming my first impression of his height. He nodded at the prizefighter vampire who went to a manhole cover in the middle of the street and lifted it up.

"What's down there?" I grimaced, picturing rats and raw sewage. I could believe a vampire like Devon would live in a filthy dark void.

"The city beneath the city." Devon walked to stand at the edge of the manhole and beckoned to me. "Come." His gaze tore through mine again and I stumbled forward, compelled.

The corporate looking vampire was the first to go down, his designer shoes clanging against the metal rungs of the ladder. Devon made me go next with a pointed look and a brusque motion of his hand. He didn't even have to talk to elicit my full cooperation. My hands gripped the cold steel ladder and my feet felt their way from rung to rung. It was colder too, the temperature dropping as the blackness below New York City swallowed me up.

Once everyone had come down, someone grabbed my elbow and guided me down a long corridor. Apparently, they could see in the dark with their super vamp eyes, which left me solely dependent on their guidance. On the upside, even though I tripped and bumbled about, at least Devon couldn't focus on me with his eyes. My head cleared somewhat as a result, but that wasn't much of an improvement since I ended up obsessing over Kristos. Was he really dead? I couldn't bring myself to believe it, yet I'd seen him fall.

We walked for quite some time, silent except for the occasional 'this way' or 'over there' comment. At last we emerged in a dimly lit underground cavern about the size of a grocery store. Exposed bedrock made up the ceiling and rows of string lights provided dim illumination. The floor underneath was dusty concrete. A tow motor sat in the distance next to several large propane tanks and disorderly rows of steel barrels.

The most noteworthy features of the subterranean landscape consisted of two construction trailers to my right. A string of construction lights hung above them, but they weren't on. As Devon thrust me in that general direction, I saw that someone had broken the light bulbs.

"Welcome to your new home," Devon said as he pushed me inside one of the trailers. The other two vampires followed and we all crammed into the small space. To my relief, someone turned on a light, allowing me to orient myself. I'd been afraid they lived like bats down there, hiding from all and any light.

On the outside the trailer had the dilapidated look of an abandoned construction site, but on the inside it was furnished with sleek leather furniture and ornate rugs. In the back, there was a bed with a crimson duvet that had the sheen of silk or satin. A chill went through me when I saw the walls, which were decked out like the torture chamber I'd found in Kristos' apartment. There were whips and floggers, chains and other things I didn't recognize although I knew what they were for: Pain.

Devon waved to the bed. "Chain her there."

The prizefighter vampire grabbed me by the wrist and dragged me toward the bed. I dug in my heels, which didn't deter him in the least. In fact, he laughed at me. A human trying to fight a vampire probably was funny...if you were the vampire.

Whether I liked it or not, he deposited me in the middle of the bed's too soft mattress. The prizefighter then yanked my arms overhead and secured them in place with chains that wrapped around and through a metal ring in the wall.

Even though I knew it was no use, I pulled on my chains anyway. On the off chance the steel was defective.

Devon came to stand at the end of the bed and gloat. He looked at me with calculated glee. "Franklin and I are going to run some errands," he said indicating the vampire in the suit. "Until then, Ivan here," he pointed to the prizefighter, "will keep an eye on you."

My eyes widened at the mention of Ivan. Wasn't that the name of the vampire that Jacques had been so terrified of? Was it possible they were one and the same? I shot a quick glance his way and he leered at me as he leaned against the wall, one hand going to caress one of the whips hanging there.

Oh god.

I closed my eyes and screamed at the connection I shared with Kristos. I poured everything I had into it, hoping to raise a response of some kind, but I sensed nothing. No one was listening on the other end of the line.

Shit.

I bit back a sob and willed myself not to cry.

Devon's face assembled into expression of mocking concern. "What's wrong, daughter? Is not the bed soft enough? I have prepared for your every comfort."

I rattled my chains, using the tension to pull myself upright. "Then let me go."

"And have to hunt you down again? That's a messy

business I would rather not repeat. You could get hurt." He sat on the edge of the bed and ran a hand up my thigh. "You are the future of the world, Myra. Together we will create a new race. You must be protected for your own good."

I couldn't keep the horror from my face. Together as in me and my father? "I don't want to make a new race."

He shook his head in disappointment. "Then you are thinking small, dear one. You are the human side of my DNA and we have the ability to do what has never been done. I will breed in you a new kind of vampire."

I recoiled at his words, wincing as their meaning hit me. A sick dread turned in my stomach. My father wanted...I couldn't even complete the thought.

Devon chuckled at my reaction. "Ah modern sensibilities are so delicate. Incest is an age-old tradition and has been used for centuries to secure a power base." His hand lingered on my thigh. "I was in Egypt when brothers married sisters. My plan is not original, I'm afraid, although my take on it is certainly unique. I think you'll find it bearable."

I made the mistake of making eye contact and his gaze caught me. The memory of Kristos using his during our lovemaking came to mind. Devon could force me to find anything enjoyable and I wouldn't be able to stop him.

Why hadn't I let Kristos turn me when I had the chance? How could I have been so stupid? The recriminations burned through me. If I got out of this alive, if I ever saw Kristos again, I would not hesitate. I couldn't afford to be human any more.

Devon squeezed my thigh and then stood up. "I'd like to stay and chat, but I have some business to attend to. Preparations must be made." He gave a wicked grin. "We're going to need a nursery down here."

15

Devon was gone for a long time. Ivan never stopped molesting me with his eyes. The only time I got a break was when he escorted me outside the trailer to a port-a-potty that appeared to be new and unused. I assumed its presence had been arranged with me in mind.

Ivan was a devious bastard. He kept my hands chained in front of me and seemed to enjoy shoving me ahead of him so hard that I stumbled. Then he would feed out lengths of chain to give me enough room to walk only bring them up short with no notice. The first few times he did this, I went sprawling in the dirt. He thought this was hilarious and guffawed loudly. I quickly caught onto his game though and was able to anticipate him and keep my feet under me.

He didn't like that and instead of staying behind me, matching my pace, he zig-zagged around me with vampire super speed. At one point, he wrapped the chain around my feet until I tripped.

"Stop it," I yelled at him, pushing myself up on all fours.

He just laughed some more and smacked me on the ass. Sick bastard.

Well two can play at this game, I thought grimly. Instead of standing I stayed on my hands and knees and crawled toward the port-a-potty. Now it was harder for him to trip me up although I would have preferred a position with more dignity.

Odd to think the last time I'd had much dignity was back before I'd become a blood courtesan. Ever since I started hanging around vampires, my life had gone to pot.

Pushing the thought away, I stood at the door to the port-a-potty, waiting.

"Go." Ivan gave the chain an impatient jerk.

I shot him a quick glare, careful not to look into his eyes long enough to be captured. "I can't do anything with my hands tied like this. Unless you want to pull down my pants for me, I suggest you untie me."

Ivan growled as he released the lock holding the chains around my wrists. "Don't try to run."

"I'm not stupid," I said. "You could outrun a car, what chance do I have?" My head held high, I entered the port-a-potty. In the process of pulling down my pants, my hand grazed the handle of the dagger. I froze for a moment. It was just me and Ivan, but was I fast enough to take him? And, if I was, would I be able to find my way out of my subterranean prison? Further, once I got out, how long could I run from my father? We had a bond that would make it easy for him to track me down again.

I fingered the dagger, debating my options.

None of them looked great. Lots of steep downsides and very little upside.

Ivan banged on the door, making the entire port-a-potty shake. I jumped and quickly finished up, yanking the jeans back over the dagger.

I washed up and then stepped outside. Ivan made to put the chains back on me, but I held up my hands. "I thought we established those weren't necessary?"

He thought it over for a second and then shrugged, casting the chains to the side. "You run, you try anything and I'll--" He raised his fist in a threatening gesture. Charming.

I cut him off. "I won't get away, I got it." I gestured to the underground cavern we stood in. "Why don't you show me around? I could use some exercise."

He bent down and snagged the chain. For a second I thought he had changed his mind and was going to restrain me again, but to my relief, he just coiled the chain around his forearm. "After we walk, I will chain you back to the bed."

I kept my face neutral not wanting to give him the satisfaction of seeing my panic. I had hoped he would abandon the chains altogether, which would give me more time to formulate a strategy. Now I had to figure something out before our little walk ended. Was I going to make a run for it or not? Time to decide was running out.

Ivan let me lead and I slowly ambled around the perimeter of the cavern. "What is this place?"

"New York underground," he said his voice short.

Well, duh. Undeterred by his lackluster response, I kept trying, "How long have you lived here?"

"We've been preparing for your arrival for the last two months."

That brought me up short. All this had been in the works long before I'd gone to Madame Rouge. My dad had known about me all this time? "How did he find me?"

Ivan smirked at me. "He's been watching you since you were born, waiting for you to be old enough to claim."

The idea of Devon lurking in the shadows of my life made me shiver. "Why now?" I asked confused. He could've taken me years ago.

A cocky half smile split Ivan's lips. "You forced his hand by becoming a blood courtesan."

I grimaced at his answer. It made sense. Daddy Dearest wanted to build a new master race with me and it wouldn't do for some other vampire to knock me up. With horror, I realized I had set this mess in motion. "So what happens next?" It was optimistic of me to ask, but I figured it didn't hurt to try. Maybe Ivan would tell me something useful.

"We bring in more trailers, then the doctors."

I looked out into the empty cavern, confused. "Doctors? What for?"

Ivan reached out and grabbed my hand. With one tug he spun me back against him. "We're going to make lots of babies, girl. Devon has promised that some of them will even be mine." Keeping a tight grip on my wrist, his other hand roamed my body, tracing the outline of my breast and then down and around to squeeze my backside.

I gave a little squeak of horror.

He smiled and pressed his lips against my throat, tongue flickering out to stroke my pulse. "If I could, I would take you to the trailer and make you bleed for me, but Devon has forbidden it."

"Just like you did to Jacques?" I asked, unable to stay silent. There was no way there were two repulsive vampires named Ivan in existence. This had to be the same guy.

Ivan chuckled. "Oh you know Jacques, do you? He was a lovely morsel but weak. His flesh was wonderful, but his spirit didn't hold up. He only lasted one night with me." Ivan kissed his way down to the hollow of my throat, his tongue applying light pressure against my windpipe. His other hand was fisted in my hair now, painfully holding me still and at his mercy.

"Something tells me you would be more fun than Jacques. You're stronger just because of your father's blood, yet still innocent enough to scream so prettily. I would break you in very quickly." He wrenched my head back even further and rested the tips of his fangs along my pulse.

My breathing quickened and I tried to push him away, but he was immovable. "I don't think my father would approve of you feeding on me," I said keeping my voice mild.

He held me in place for a long moment and then abruptly let me go. I stumbled and dropped to one knee as I lost my balance.

My hand went to the hilt of the dagger. "When will my father return?" I pulled the dagger out of its sheath and keeping it hidden against my side, I pushed myself back up to my feet. A loose plan began to take shape in my mind.

"It's four hours until sunrise," he said his voice strained. He wasn't really paying attention to me and appeared more focused on gaining control of his own blood lust.

"He'll be gone that long?" I infused my voice with surprise trying to hide the relief that I would have so much time.

Ivan gave a curt nod.

Hoping the vampire had more blood lust than brains, I walked over to him, my hips swaying seductively as I went. He froze as I approached, confusion flashing across his face. I smiled and bit my lip in an effort to sell the lie I was about to tell. The small gesture always ignited Kristos' desire and I hoped Ivan wasn't immune. From the way his gaze locked on my mouth, he wasn't. Good. I needed him to forget that just a minute ago I'd wanted nothing to do with him.

I put a hand up to his neck and pulled him close. "Maybe when my father is done with all this master race business you and I could..." I trailed off and kissed him.

His arms wrapped around my waist and he groaned against my lips. Before I could lose my nerve, I thrust the dagger into his eye as fast and as hard as I could.

He fought me during the few seconds it took for the dagger to breach his brain. One hand clawed around my neck and squeezed until it felt like my head would pop off. His other hand yanked on my hair threatening to scalp me with brutal strength alone.

With a garbled yelp, I pressed the button. Immediately he went limp and fell to the ground, mouth open in a silent scream. For a moment, I just stood there hand on my throat, trying to take in what I'd just done. Then, with grim determination I went to where he lay and sliced the edge of the dagger against his throat. Black blood oozed up like tar, but I didn't stop. I couldn't chance Ivan telling Devon what had happened or coming after me. I had to make a clean getaway. So I sawed and hacked at his head until I separated it from his body. My wrists throbbed with the effort by the time I was done and I was pretty sure I would be sore later.

With Ivan dispatched, I wiped the dagger on his pants along with my hands and then dragged his body off behind a trailer. I'd thought that maybe vampires turned to dust when they died, but if they did, it was a slow process. Ivan's head I just kicked and rolled along to the spot where I'd dropped his body. I didn't want to leave any obvious evidence. Let Devon wonder what had happened.

The last thing I did before I left, was lift Ivan's wallet. There wasn't much cash in there, about fifty bucks, but between that and the credit cards I should be able to get somewhere.

I ventured into the dark tunnels that had brought me to Devon's lair, pausing to quickly vomit. While I'd handled Ivan's decapitation better than Arlo's, my stomach was still delicate about the whole thing.

With one hand on the wall and the dagger clutched in the other, I tried to remember the twists and turns we'd taken on our way down. It didn't matter if I found the exact manhole we'd used, I just needed to find a way out, any way out would do. I was way past being picky.

Please just let me get out of here and somehow find a place to hide where Devon can't find me.

What seemed like forever later, I got lucky. I could hear traffic overhead and a metallic clang as vehicles bounced over what I decided must be a loose manhole cover. Picking up my pace, I tracked the sound and sighed with relief when my hand bumped into the rungs of a ladder. I sheathed the dagger and began to climb.

Something heavy rumbled overhead, a truck or a bus, and I winced as the vibrations telegraphed from the street down the ladder. It sounded like I'd found a busy street, maybe too busy for me to safely climb out of the manhole.

At the top of the ladder, I pressed both hands against the cool metal of the manhole cover and pushed. It shifted ever so slightly, but resisted my efforts to lift it up and to the side. A horn blared and the weight of a car passed directly above me. More horns sounded along with screeching wheels and then a truck lumbered through.

I thought about moving on and looking for another way out versus poking my head out of the ground for a game of human Frogger. Neither option sounded appealing, but I decided I would at least get the manhole cover off so I could see what my options were. Or weren't as the case may be.

Mustering all my strength I heaved the cover up. I wasn't strong enough to lift it, but I could raise it high enough to tip it over. It rolled off the hole and dropped to the street with a booming clang. I risked a peek out and promptly ducked as a delivery truck came barreling down on me. I watched it pass over head along with the steady stream of cars that followed, wondering how the hell I was going to climb out without being hit.

At least I'd managed to catch a glimpse of my location, but that didn't mean I had any idea where I was. I knew so little of New York City's geography that my ignorance might actually end up killing me at some point. All I could tell was that I'd managed to find a very busy road.

I risked another peek and realized I was next to a crosswalk, one with a light. At some point there would be a red light and the traffic would stop. I just had to wait it out.

It was the longest light in history.

I could have grown and harvested crops in the time it took for the light to go red. It probably had something to do with the tiny cross street that had hardly any traffic. When the light finally changed, I started the process of hoisting myself up. Despite all the people milling about, no one gave me a second glance. This also meant no one offered to help. Giving the throng of people a dirty look, I pulled my torso out and planted one knee on the pavement preparing to pull the rest of me out.

At the same time, a phantom hand grabbed my ankle and with one powerful yank I was falling back into darkness.

I screamed even though I knew no one would come rushing to save me. I couldn't help myself. The freefall only lasted a few seconds though and I landed in the hard embrace of strange arms.

"Going somewhere, daughter?" The low hiss of my father's voice filled my ears. He squeezed me tight. "You thought I wouldn't notice Ivan was gone? You've been blood bound to how many of us now and still don't understand how it works?"

I remained silent even though he shook me a bit. Fear and anger crashed through me, vying for space. I had come so close to escape only to fail. The damn blood bond would be my downfall so long as my father was alive. I thought of the dagger then and my fingers flexed, involuntarily reaching for it.

Maybe I had to die, but now I knew my father did too.

Keeping a tight grip on my arm, he dragged me back through the dark labyrinth to his lair, which had become a hive of activity while I was gone. Two new trailers had arrived and there were people there unpacking all sorts of equipment. One box was labeled ultrasound equipment and several others bore the name of a pharmaceutical company. They must've come in from another tunnel system as I'd neither seen nor heard them during my getaway attempt.

"What's happening?" I asked as he shoved me back toward the trailer I'd been imprisoned in earlier.

"My plan is falling into place. You see, I've found a way to be efficient." He smiled, lips curling into sharp points on either side of his angular face. "You have one womb but many eggs. With a hundred surrogates, I will have a small army within twenty years."

"You're going to take my eggs?" My eyes went wide. I hadn't seen this coming. Egg donor to vampires was not something I'd ever thought to add to my resume.

"As many as I can get. One hundred just to start." He waved a hand toward a group of men in surgical scrubs. "I have a medical team all set."

"What do they think they're doing? Did you tell them the truth?"

"No of course not. It's a secret government project with generous funding. Patriotism and money lower the ethical bar so that no one asks too many questions." We had arrived at the trailer now and he opened the door. Before I knew it, I was tied up on the bed again.

I yanked on my chains even though I knew they would hold. I couldn't help myself. "Where are you getting the surrogates?"

He crossed his arms and leaned against the wall, completely relaxed as if he hatched evil diabolical plans on a regular basis. Given what I'd seen so far, he probably did. "Why so many questions, daughter? Surely the details don't interest you?"

"Just trying to understand," I said lamely. In truth, I hoped to learn something that would help me escape again.

"Well, if you must know, the surrogates have been harder to find than you. It's a niche industry. I couldn't find enough to pay for their services so I've resorted to recruiting women with my own methods." He winked at me and my stomach sank when I realized he had captured them with his eyes.

"Where are they now?" I hadn't seen any of these women in the lair, just an assortment of medical professionals and people carrying boxes.

"They'll be here when we need them," he said. "Right now, we're focusing on getting you to make as many eggs as possible for our project."

I grimaced suddenly feeling like a prize mare. Pulling on my bonds again—it was beginning to be a compulsion—I said, "You don't have to tie me up. It's not like you can't find me wherever I go." I held my breath hoping the ruse would work a second time.

He shook his head. "Maybe if you hadn't killed Ivan I would have considered it, but you showed your hand there, daughter. You're too ruthless for me to turn loose. I'll keep my head, thank you very much." He put a hand in his pocket. "Oh and I found something you might like to see." He tossed a crumpled piece of newspaper on the bed.

I squinted at it. "What is it?"

"A news story about your protector Kristos. I know you think you'll see him again and it seems he did survive the car accident." He flashed an evil grin and adjusted the chains holding my hands overhead so that I could rest them at my side and reach the newspaper. "Read it and understand, you are mine." He leaned over me then and planted a kiss on my cheek, his mouth cold and hard.

I cringed, my lips curling in disgust, but he was gone before I could say anything. With a sigh I smoothed out the newspaper. He'd said Kristos had survived, but, as much as hope filled my heart, I had a strange feeling that wasn't good news. Daddy Dearest had been too happy about it, which didn't make any sense.

It turned out my instincts were right. Kristos may not have died when my father snatched me, but he did not live much past that moment. My heart sank when I saw a picture of a fireball in the sky. A caption underneath said, "CEO Kristos Anastos died yesterday in a helicopter crash near the site of Med Enterprises' new headquarters."

My chest convulsed as if I'd been hit and tears dripped from my eyes. *Had Kristos been trying to find me?*

The article went on to say that he'd held a short press conference about the new building and the company's hopes for its future home. Then he'd boarded a helicopter which exploded for some unknown reason. Police and the FAA were investigating, but foul play was not suspected.

Hands shaking, I smoothed the newspaper over and over, finding the repetition soothing. I hadn't felt our bond since the car accident, but I'd held out hope that he was still out there looking for me. I knew he could survive a bullet, but an explosion wouldn't leave anything behind to regenerate.

I had to face reality: Kristos was gone.

Oh God.

I balled up the newspaper and threw it as hard as I could. "Damn it." The tears kept pouring out, a silent procession of pain. I scrubbed at my eyes with my fists trying to stuff it all back in. This was not the time to fall apart. Not if I wanted to survive.

I took in a deep breath and slowly exhaled as I considered my options. Mostly I didn't have any so long as I was kept tied up and so long as my nightmare of a father was alive. I would never be free until he was dead.

But how to kill him with my hands tied?

I still had my dagger. Somehow they'd missed it not once but twice now. I had some slack in the chains around my wrists, but I didn't have the strength of a vampire. I'd gotten lucky with Ivan, managing to find a weak spot that I could use to distract him.

But my father didn't want my body, he just wanted my eggs. Probably the last thing he would want to do is knock me up with old-fashioned sex, it would ruin his plans. So that meant seduction was out. To boot, I had a feeling the rest of me was disposable and if I wasn't careful I would outlive my usefulness once his little baby army had launched.

Once I was used up, what would he do with me? Make me a vampire? My gut said he wouldn't want that. Yeah, I might be under his control for however long, but I would fight him tooth and nail. My escape earlier was just a hint of the hell I would raise and I doubted he'd missed that fact. Not much incentive for him to make me stronger and faster.

With those thoughts swirling around in my head, I drifted into a light sleep, the exhaustion of the night's events finally catching up to me.

16

Much later, I woke with a start when a heavy hand covered my mouth. Instantly my eyes went wide and I flailed, my hands trying to peel the fingers off my mouth. They were as strong as iron and immovable, which meant only one thing; Vampire.

"Myra, shh," came a familiar voice. "It's me." The hand lifted and my mouth was free.

Blinking I stared at a wishful dream. He couldn't be real. Kristos was dead. There was no way he could be standing there, but I reached a hand out anyway and touched him. He was solid as a wall.

"Kristos, is it really you?" I whispered.

He nodded.

He looked tired, I noted. His skin was even paler than usual as if he hadn't fed in a long time, but his eyes brimmed with their usual vampire Jedi mind tricks. Once again, I felt as if I was in a free fall; my body moving up, my stomach dropping down like a roller coaster hitting the crest of a hill just before it hurtled back down to earth.

"I thought you were dead. I couldn't feel you." I ran a hand along his shoulder, my eyes wide with wonder.

"My death was staged. I had plans to do the same for you, but then the car accident..." He trailed off and made a helpless gesture with his hands. "As for our blood bond, the bedrock is like static. It provides enough interference to make it hard to track anyone, let alone tell if they're alive. I've been searching for you since you were taken and didn't feel you until last night."

I nodded. "I tried to escape. I made it to street level before Devon caught me." For whatever reason the bedrock hadn't interfered with Devon's signal. Maybe linked DNA made for a stronger bond.

"Has he fed from you?" Kristos reached out and tilted my chin up examining my neck.

I shook my head. "No."

"Good." He reached up and ripped the metal ring out of the wall as if it was a knife cutting soft butter. "Let's go."

I balked. "No."

My resistance surprised him. "If we don't go now, I'm not sure we'll get out. It's almost dusk, Myra."

I shook my head. "You don't understand. The rules are different between us. He doesn't have to take blood from me to bind me. I *am* his blood. He'll find me wherever we run."

He blinked as he considered my words. With a decisive nod, he said, "You're right. You may not be a vampire, but you have enough of his blood to be bound to him."

I looked up at Kristos. "We have to kill him or I'll never be safe."

"Do you know where he sleeps during the day?" Kristos went to a window in the trailer and pulled aside the shade to peer out into the underground cavern. "We have to find him before he wakes. He's stronger than me."

I shrugged. "He has to be here somewhere. He's spent too much time building this to not sleep here. Besides he won't want to be far from me, especially after I almost got away." Struck by the memory of how my bond with Kristos had been a two-way connection, I said, "Wait a second. Let me try something." I closed my eyes and searched for the link between my father and me. It didn't come as naturally to me as the bond with Kristos, but I did find it. I had to think of how much he creeped me out, how afraid I was of him to bring it to life. The bond throbbed within me like an unwanted blood blister and the sensation made me wince.

Raising a hand, I pointed. "He's out there. I think I can find him."

Lacking a key and, apparently, the strength to break steel, Kristos draped the chains around my neck and we left the trailer. The underground cavern appeared to be deserted, although I knew better. There had to be other vampires down here, the stillness just meant they weren't awake yet. The sun kept them at bay for the moment, but night would be here soon. Too soon for me to dawdle. Breathing in the damp, subterranean air, I closed my eyes and held my hand out like a dowsing rod.

Following the pull of the invisible strand linking me to my father, I led Kristos to a dark corner of the underground hide-out. There was no trailer here, but a small shed, the kind people used to store lawnmowers. Given the lack of grass underground, I didn't doubt its true purpose was more nefarious. I tried to open the door, but found it locked.

Kristos motioned for me to step aside and simply tore the door off its hinges. Inside, my father lay on a small bed, hands folded neatly over his chest as if he was ready for his funeral. I pulled the dagger out of its sheath and made to step inside, but Kristos held me back.

"Let me do it, I'm faster and stronger."

I wanted to protest, but he was right so I handed over the dagger.

Kristos did the blurry run thing vampires do when they move faster than the human eye can track them. In less than a second, before my heart could even finish a full beat, the dagger was thrust into my father's brain.

He shuddered as the holy water melted his central nervous system but, to my immense relief, didn't wake. Kristos removed the dagger and used it to hack at his neck same as I had done to Ivan, except being stronger, it only took him about thirty seconds.

I watched my father's head roll off the bed and thud to the ground with a sense of both horror and satisfaction. It was done. He was dead. I didn't have a father once again, only this time I was happy about it.

"This is too easy," I whispered to myself unable to believe this nightmare was over. I looked over my shoulder half expecting to see Devon there, a mocking smile twisting his lips, but the cavern yawned behind me, empty and silent.

Kristos wiped the dagger clean and handed it back to me. "The old ones think they are invincible and that leads to mistakes. I would have never been so exposed in my sleep, but Devon probably believed he was untouchable."

Clumsy from the press of the chains on my shoulders, I pulled out the flask of holy water and worked to refill the dagger. "He really thought you were dead and that no one was coming after me."

Kristos shrugged. "That was his first mistake. I am not an old one, but I've survived longer than most. Devon underestimated me." He paused to reach out and take the dagger from me, holding it for me while I put the lid back on the flask of holy water. "His second mistake was forgetting I could walk during the day."

"Thank God for mistakes," I murmured tucking the flask into the small of my back and holding my hand out for the dagger. I quickly sheathed the weapon and then eased the chains off my shoulders, letting them fall to the ground. Their weight made my neck ache. "By the way, I think the key for these might be in his pocket."

He nodded and went to look. I watched as he rummaged through the dead vampire's pockets, grateful that I couldn't see much gore from my current viewpoint. My stomach was not as delicate about vampire decapitation anymore, but I didn't want to provoke it.

A second later Kristos pulled the key from Devon's pocket and quickly unlocked the chains, which fell off my wrists and hit the ground with a sharp clang. Together, we turned to leave the shed and then froze as we heard a voice call out, "Devon?"

Kristos looked at me, concern in his eyes. "It's dusk."

Which meant we weren't alone and this wasn't over yet.

"What do we do?" I whispered.

"Run." He grabbed my hand and pulled me after him.

We skirted the shadows around the perimeter of the cavern, aiming for the opening that would take us into the maze of underground tunnels. Before we could slip away into darkness, someone found my father's remains and the alarm went out. The place was crawling with people now. Judging by the smooth fluidity and speed of their movements, they were probably all vampires, way more than I'd ever seen before. Devon must have called them in as backup while I was stuck in the trailer.

I looked at Kristos with wide eyes and he gave my hand a reassuring squeeze. "Don't panic, no one's seen us yet."

Just as he finished saying that, a cry went out. We'd been spotted. Franklin, the vampire who'd been with Devon when he first captured me, zoomed over to us, his face a feral mask of fanged anger. He wrapped his hands around my throat and tried to drag me away with him. I twisted in his grasp, hoping this would be the one time I managed to overcome vampire super strength. Sadly, I didn't break free and instead hit my head against a piece of jagged stone sticking out of the wall.

Stars exploded behind my eyelids and I just stood there blinking stupidly while Kristos kicked the vampire in the stomach with enough force that he had to let me go or lose his balance. Of course, that didn't stop him for long and he came right back at me. Kristos stepped between us and smashed his fist into Franklin's nose.

Snatching up my hand again, Kristos took off dragging me behind him. My brain was still too scrambled to process everything that had happened let alone keep up with the pace Kristos had set. I stumbled and fell, gravel biting into the palm of my hand.

Kristos muttered a swear word under his breath and scooped me up like a helpless baby. Cradling me in his arms, he did his best to run, but there was no denying I slowed him down. Franklin not only caught up to us, but passed us by and turned around to face us head on.

Kristos slowed down. "Devon's gone, let us go."

Franklin sneered. "Devon may be dead, but his plan is very much alive. I'm not letting her go. Not until she fulfills her purpose."

He rushed Kristos, forcing him to drop me. I hit the ground, crying out as my spine slammed into hard rock. My head took another hit too and felt like a bruised melon. Kristos and Franklin fought like a UFC match on fast forward. Everything was a blur of violence that moved too fast for me to see it properly.

Kristos smashed Franklin's head against the wall. I blinked and they were rolling on the ground. Their fighting stirred up dust and spit out rocks as they scuffled in the dirt. The other vampires had spotted us now and circled around, advancing on me.

I pushed myself into a sitting position and crab walked back to the wall so there was something solid at my back. Brandishing the dagger, I said, "Stay back."

A tall, lean vampire wearing a black motorcycle jacket advanced on me. "You think a knife will stop us?"

"It stopped Devon, didn't it?" I flashed a smile meant to show I wasn't afraid. "Did you want to follow in his footsteps?"

He paused mid-step, gaze searching my face as if he wasn't sure of the truth. I averted my eyes to avoid being captured and caught sight of another vampire sidling up to me from the opposite direction. They weren't the only ones either. I was outnumbered easily twelve to one.

Shit.

"Kristos," I called out. "You might want to finish up."

Kristos paused for a second, his arm wrapped around Franklin in a headlock and took in my predicament. He gave a curt nod and tore Franklin's head off. Then he whirled around and ran off...away from me.

"Kristos," I screamed. What the hell was he doing? He hadn't stood by me this long to abandon me to my fate now.

The other vampires laughed, pleased to see that my sole

protector had disappeared. They started to close in on me faster. My heart pounded in my chest and my breathing quickened. This was the end. There was no more escape.

One of them leaped for me and even though the guy was a blur of super speed, I managed to lodge the dagger into the vampire's belly before he laid a hand on me. Apparently it didn't bother him much because he just smiled, but then I pressed the button, flooding his gut with holy water. That got his attention and he fell to the ground, screaming.

"Who's next?" I asked, my voice full of fake bravado. I'd managed to refill the dagger after we'd killed Devon, but there was no way I had enough holy water to take on everyone. I was in a fight I couldn't win. Maybe that was why Kristos had run off, although I couldn't believe he would desert me after everything we'd been through.

The remaining vamps all looked at each other, uneasy, but I was too tempting a morsel and they came closer yet. A female vampire with blond buzz cut hair reached for me next. I batted her hand away with the dagger, and when she was close enough, I gasped as I recognized her. "Samira?"

She snickered. "I thought maybe you had forgotten about me."

"Was my Dad your master?" I asked curious to know if that's who'd been pulling her puppet strings.

"No," came the short reply and then she lunged for me.

I jumped back and managed to sink the dagger into her eye

as it widened in surprise. There was a popping sensation as the blade broke through her eyeball to the soft brain beneath. With a certain amount of satisfaction I hit the holy water button. "Pay back's a bitch," I said remembering how she'd kidnapped my mother and then tried to take me.

Samira was too far gone to say anything. She began to twitch as her nerves melted. Losing control of her body, she fell back, her face a twisted mask of pain. Sagging to the ground, she flailed there like a turtle flipped on its back.

The other vampires hesitated now. They had me cornered and were stronger and faster than me, there was no denying that, but how to catch me without risking a hit had them stumped. Lucky for me, I don't think any of them knew I was out of holy water. My little moment of revenge had led me to hold the button down longer than necessary, giving Samira an extra big dose. If I had more than a teaspoon left, it would be a true miracle.

A motorcycle sputtered in the distance, the sound causing the vampires to look at each other in confusion. The tunnels under New York were not a place anyone expected a biker rally. We all turned to look toward its source as it roared louder and louder. Kristos zoomed into Devon's lair on a sleek black motorcycle and turned toward us. Raising one hand, he aimed a gun at the vampires surrounding me and began to shoot with unerring accuracy.

Pop-pop-pop. Heads exploded around me, bursting like bloody fruit.

I cowered on the ground not wanting to sustain collateral damage, which always seemed to be my specialty in these situations. The motorcycle came to a stop in front of me, purring like an angry lion.

"Get on," Kristos shouted.

I nodded and started to clamber onto the bike behind him. Just as I was about to settle into the seat rough hands grabbed me and yanked me back.

I screamed and thrashed, trying to break free, but the grip was strong as steel. A gun muzzle pressed against the side of my head.

"Be still," barked an angry voice in my ear.

I froze, as did Kristos.

"You're not the only one with a gun, Kristos," said the vampire who held me. "You have to shoot her to get to me. Doesn't sound like a good plan."

"Let her go and I'll let you live," said Kristos his voice dark and tight. His eyes never left mine and I felt him stir inside my head.

"Go away and I'll let *you* live," countered the vampire.

"What are you going to do with her?"

The vampire squeezed me. "That's none of your business, but I'm sure you can imagine. A child of The Maker would make a good bride."

"I'll kill you the first chance I get," I hissed.

That made my captor laugh. "You can try, little girl. I'll

enjoy punishing you for your transgressions. Or maybe I'll just keep you naked and tied up for my convenience. Or perhaps I'll whore you out to the highest bidder."

I closed my eyes and shuddered. If that was the future that awaited me, let me die here and now. I opened my eyes and stared hard into Kristos' as I mouthed the words 'do it.'

Next thing I knew, Kristos had stormed into my head with his gaze. The invasion hurt and I gasped, but quickly realized he was giving me instructions. He wanted me to lean to the side to try and give him a clear shot. It was going to be Arlo all over again. I lunged against the arms holding me, hoping just this once to be strong enough to take on a vampire. The vampire's grip on me loosened a fraction and I shifted maybe a half inch in the direction Kristos had wanted me to go.

That must've been all Kristos needed as he took the shot. Suddenly I was free and running to leap onto the back of the bike. I didn't look back to see what had happened to the vampire, but I knew he wasn't incapacitated when a bullet ripped across my side.

I screamed and arched back as another bullet grazed my temple. Tightening my arms around Kristos, I shouted, "Go, go."

He hit the gas and the motorcycle bucked between our legs as it shot forward. I prayed we were faster than a vampire on foot. Prayed this nightmare would end before I died. I was losing blood. It oozed through my shirt wetting my skin so that the breeze felt cold.

"I'm hit," I yelled.

Kristos nodded that he heard me and made the bike go even faster. We were in the tunnels now and I couldn't see anything in the dark. My arms began to shake along with the rest of me as the injuries I'd sustained took their toll. I was losing my strength along with my blood and pain wracked my body.

"We have to stop," I said, but I couldn't make my voice loud enough to be heard. Closing my eyes, I pushed myself into the bond hoping to get his attention that way.

"It's not safe yet. Hang on," he said over his shoulder. He moved but I couldn't see what he was doing. It felt like he was searching his pockets for something. Then I saw a little red light in his hand. He was holding something. As I watched, the light went from red to green and a loud boom sounded behind us. I looked over my shoulder to see a strange lightning flash underground.

Kristos took a hard right just as a ball of flame rolled down the tunnel after us. Its heat licked at my back. I cowered against him. It took everything in me not to lose my hold on him and fall off the bike, bouncing into the darkness.

The ground beneath us changed, rising up instead of being flat, and a moment later, we flew out of an access tunnel into the night. I sagged against Kristos as he brought the bike to a stop.

"What was that?" I looked back into the tunnel, expecting to see flames, but there was only quiet darkness. You would never guess there'd been a baby factory in process down there somewhere. Or that it had just all gone kablooey.

"There were propane tanks. I rigged a bomb." He turned off

the bike and put down the kickstand.

"Oh. So is that where you went?" Kristos never ceased to amaze me. He always had a plan. Too bad this last one didn't look like it would work out so well for me.

"Yes." He swung his leg off the bike and started to examine my injuries.

"I thought you left me." I tried to get off the bike too, but instead of standing, I sank down to the ground. I couldn't feel my legs so much anymore and more blood gushed out of the wound in my back.

"I took a risk. We were outnumbered and needed to change the game. I would never leave you, Myra. I thought I was fast enough." A grimace of regret flashed across his face.

"You were fast enough, but I think I might be leaving you anyway," I said dully. I wasn't a doctor, but even I knew it wasn't good that my limbs had gone numb. My vision was cloudy as well, full of dark spots that only allowed me a partial view of Kristos. He was so damn handsome it made my heart ache.

"No, Myra, not yet," he said gently helping me stand.

But he didn't have any say in the matter. A strange, weary heaviness filled me and I felt my heart stutter in my chest. There wasn't much time now. "I'm sorry, Kristos." I put a hand on his cheek wanting to touch him one last time. He'd worked so hard to save me and I was going to die anyway. "I'll miss you."

He gently lowered me to the ground. "Hush. It's all right."

I wanted to ask him how. I was about to die the kind of

death no one woke up from. There was no going back now. "I should've changed a long time ago," I managed to gasp out. "I was afraid. I didn't know what I wanted."

Kristos put a finger to my lips. "I know. I'm sorry it turned out this way."

"Me too." Breathing hurt now, forcing me to take smaller and smaller breaths. My eyes drifted shut despite my efforts to keep them open. I could feel the darkness opening up and preparing to swallow me. I thought of my mom with a pang. Would she be okay without me?

"My mom," I whispered.

"I'll see to her," Kristos said.

I couldn't see him anymore even though I managed to open my eyes. There was just darkness now, nothing else, but his hand squeezed mine. I was alive, barely, but still there and he was with me. That made it better.

Then the dark washed over me in an unstoppable wave, sweeping me out into oblivion as it passed. I knew nothing more.

17

I was rocking. A soft, lulling motion that jostled me into consciousness. I tried to open my eyes, but it was too hard. I gave up and retreated into nothingness. The rocking brought me back, but I couldn't break through the heaviness holding me down to fully awaken.

Time passed. Somehow I knew that. There were sounds now with the rocking. Jazzy music. Doors opening and closing. A ticking sound that I found irritating.

A hand touched me, squeezing my shoulder gently.

I groaned.

"Sleep," whispered a voice that instantly reassured me. I obediently drifted off, dreamless except for disconnected flashes of Kristos bent over me, concern on his face. In one of them I felt his fangs pierce my neck followed by the draw of him sucking my blood and it seemed I could hear him calling my name over and over. Whether they were memories or hallucinations, I couldn't say. I didn't have the energy to fret about it either. All I could do was drift, lost in myself.

The next time I woke, I was cuddled around someone. My eyes opened this time. Before they snapped closed again, I caught sight of a car backseat and felt the press of someone next to me. Outside it was dusk.

Something wet and warm pressed against my mouth. "Drink," came the soft command.

I drank, hesitant sips at first which soon gave way to giant greedy gulps. Blood filled my mouth, rousing my hunger. The need to eat roared to life with a ferocity that would've frightened me if I hadn't been in a stupor. It tasted so good, I moaned as I drank.

"Enough. Sleep."

I whimpered in protest and fell asleep again.

"Myra, wake." The deep voice rushed my ears and shivered through my body.

I woke fully this time and sat up. I was still in the back seat of a car, an unknown driver at the front. We raced down an unknown highway. It was dusk again or maybe still, I couldn't tell. Palm trees and ocean streamed by in a surreal vacation landscape.

I looked to the man who had spoken. He looked calm and composed as ever. "Kristos?" My voice was slurred. My mouth felt funny, like I'd had a dozen root canals back-to-back.

"Yes." He pulled me against his chest as I began to slump, weak as a newborn kitten.

"What happened?"

"You died." He kissed the top of my head. "And now you live again."

I was silent for several long minutes. "You changed me." The little flashes I'd seen in my dreams must have been memories then.

I felt his nod. "Yes."

"Is it over now?" I tensed afraid he would say no.

"I think so. The council believes us both to be dead. No one is looking for us."

"Madame Rouge? She's probably furious with me." I'd left her in the lurch and never really did my job like I was supposed to; the bullets kept getting in the way.

Kristos gave me a little shake. "You're dead remember? She has the same information as the council does. You don't need to worry about her."

"What about my mom?" Panic flashed through me. How long had I been out? Was mom okay? Oh my God. Why hadn't she been the first thing on my mind? Guilt burned through me although I knew I wasn't myself. I wasn't exactly thinking straight. I felt like I'd awakened after a long fight with the flu; sore and fuzzy around the edges.

"She's home. Cancer free." He held up a hand and said, "Before you ask, no she has no idea what's happened. As far as she knows you're still working at an internship."

I smiled, pleased at the news. By some miracle we'd both survived. "Can I see her?" I held my breath. Could I see her again?

Was that allowed? Oh the irony of losing her this way when I'd been so afraid it would be the cancer that would take her from me.

"After a time, yes." He shifted in his seat, drawing me even closer to him.

His response made me frown. "I thought that I would have to leave her behind." Especially now that no one could know I'd survived.

He sighed, patient with me yet suffering through all my questions. "This isn't fiction, Myra. This is real vampire life. We don't leave our loved ones behind unless we have to."

"But what happens when they notice you don't age or die?"

He tapped the side of his eye. "You'll mesmerize her so she'll only remember what you want her to. And when she dies, you step away to be forgotten. No one will look twice if you are careful."

My eyes narrowed. "Hey, I thought you said the eye thing didn't work like that." I was newly risen from the dead, not afflicted with Alzheimer's. He'd said he couldn't make people do things. I remembered that conversation well because it had eased my mind a great deal.

He lifted a shoulder in a half shrug. "I downplayed its power a bit."

Despite the languid weakness in my limbs, I managed to smack his shoulder.

Kristos winced. "That reaction is precisely why I kept quiet. It's not like I can turn it off and I really did try to tone it down. You have to admit there were times where it was a distinct asset."

I rolled my eyes, but let it go because he was right. I'd enjoyed his gaze more than once. Of course if he set those baby blues on me going forward we would have some serious words and my smacks would get a whole lot stronger. "Where are we going now?" I gestured to the passing scenery.

"Someplace safe." The car slowed as he spoke, aiming for the upcoming exit.

"Will we always have to hide?" I rested my head on his shoulder, contemplating the palm trees outside.

He shrugged. "We will reinvent ourselves. After a century or so they will forget."

The idea of a hundred years gave me pause. I would be twenty-five forever. I gave Kristos a sly look. "I'm the same flavor for eternity."

He smiled, eyes crinkling at the corners. "Yes, the one that reminded my heart what it was to feel again. That's a pretty special flavor if you ask me. Besides, I have no doubt you'll spice things up."

Sudden concern flashed through me. I pressed a hand to my stomach. "What if..." I stopped, unable to say the words.

He took my hand and kissed it. "Your father was unique among vampires. You may take after him or not. We will be happy no matter what."

The car lurched as it made a sharp turn into a residential

area, throwing me against him. I became aware of Kristos in a new way as a sudden heat throbbed in my core. I threaded my fingers in his hair and pulled him to my lips for a kiss.

He indulged me, tongue lashing mine and flicking over my new fangs which were sharp as a viper's. I was a clumsy kisser now, unable to gauge where my fangs were. Afraid of nicking Kristos or myself, I held still and let him control our kiss. He sucked on my bottom lip until I moaned at the sensation. Then the car slowed to a stop and he pulled away saying, "We're here."

He opened the car door and stepped out into the humid night. I followed and learned that 'here' was an immense house by the sea. The bright moon hung overhead and the sound of waves breaking on the nearby beach welcomed us. My senses were sharper now. I could smell the salt in the soft breeze dancing around me, and I heard what sounded like heart beats that strummed like hummingbird wings.

I cocked my head and listened. "Do you hear that?"

Kristos smiled and, with a start, I realized I could see him in sharp relief despite the absence of direct light. Well, hello there vampire super powers.

"Yes. You'll learn to tune it out eventually."

Kristos dispatched the driver, who left with a tip of his chauffeur's hat and then grabbed my hand, tugging me after him into the stucco house. I had a second to notice the sweeping marbled entrance with its crystal chandelier before he was on me. His lips burned mine and his hands roamed over me, pulling off my clothes.

My body responded instantly to his touch and I gave a happy sigh. He fisted his hands in my hair and buried his face in my neck.

"Myra," he whispered my name with longing.

"Is everything okay?" I pulled back to look at him.

His gaze was solemn as it met mine and for once I didn't feel the pull of his vampire eyes. "I wasn't sure you would change."

"I thought I was dead too." I gestured to my body. "But here I am. We make a pretty good team, don't we?" I unbuttoned his shirt as I spoke revealing his always magnificent chest.

He sighed as I touched him, shuddering slightly when my palms grazed his nipples. "We are lucky to have survived."

"Let's find a bed and put that luck to work." I grabbed his hand and pulled him after me up the stairs. I had a million questions now that I was a vampire. How would I feed? Would I take after my father? Or would I favor Kristos since he was my maker? What would I tell my mother? More importantly, how would I spend my time now that it wasn't running out?

As pressing as the questions were, I had all the time in the world to find answers. Just then I wanted to press my body against Kristos' and lose myself in his eyes. That seemed a fitting way to mark the day I rose from the dead. We could play twenty questions later.

He seemed to agree as he took me into a bedroom and

loved me until I could barely remember my name.

"Hey Kristos?" I said during a break between orgasms.

"Yes, love." He toyed with my breasts, taunting my nipples until they went stiff in protest.

I sighed and arched up toward him. "I love you." I'd had to die and rise again to realize it, but Kristos was my everything. If I had him, I was complete. Nothing else mattered.

Kristos smiled at me. "I love you too, Myra."

"You do?" My jaw dropped. "I thought you didn't like female vampires?"

"I thought I didn't like a lot of things about relationships. You made me reconsider."

"When did you know?" I smiled up at him and caressed the broad planes of his pecs.

"From the beginning." He dipped his head down and sucked my mouth into a tender kiss.

"That explains a lot," I mumbled against his lips thinking of his attentive loyalty and concern for my safety. "Here I thought you were a gentleman."

"I'm no gentleman." He covered my body with his and took me roughly to prove it. I shuddered under him and for once, there were no bullets, just blissful release.

***

Thank you for reading! I hope you enjoyed Reborn which is part of the Blood Courtesans series. Reviews are always appreciated! Don't forget to visit www.bloodcourtesans.com!

ABOUT THE AUTHOR

NY Times and USA Today Bestselling author Michelle Fox lives in the Midwest with her husband, kids, the occasional exchange student and two, sweetly disobedient dogs. She loves fantasy and romance, which makes writing paranormal romance a natural fit. Occasionally, she goes through a maverick phase and writes contemporary romance. In her spare time, she's been known to shake her bon-bon at Zumba, make spectacular cheesecakes, hoard vintage costume jewelry and eat way too much ice cream (Ben and Jerry's Karamel Sutra for the win!).

Made in the USA
Middletown, DE
04 March 2021